SHE FELL FOR A BOSS 3

A Novel By
KC MILLS

© **2016**

Published by Leo Sullivan Presents
www.leolsullivan.com

Chapter One

Yami woke up with an eerie feeling running through her that intensified when she noticed that she was in bed alone. After reaching for her cellphone, she checked the time and realized that it was almost two in the morning.

With no calls or texts from Miego, she began to panic because that wasn't like him, especially since he had only planned to be gone for a few hours. Here it was almost two in the morning and he wasn't home and hadn't tried to contact her.

The first thing she did was try his phone. It went straight to voicemail, so she tried again and got the same thing. Not knowing what else to do, she climbed out of bed and searched the house, praying that this was one of the nights when he couldn't sleep and was in his studio.

She knew before she even pushed the door open and found it empty that he wasn't in there, but she had to try anyway. Her next move was to inspect the rest of their apartment, which was dark and quiet. After sticking her head in Ray's door, where she found her daughter balled up in the center of the bed with her thumb in her mouth, Yami made her way to the living room. No Miego, and no sign that he had been there. Everything was just as she left it when she finally decided to call it a night.

Just that quickly, her pulse was racing and her heart rate had increased to a quicker steady pace that had her feeling short of breath. Not knowing what else to do, she dialed Train, hoping that he had some answers. Maybe Miego had crashed there for whatever reason. She'd be pissed if that were the case, but relieved that he was okay.

"Yeah."

Train's voice was groggy and heavy, so she knew that she had just woke him up.

"Hey, sorry to wake you, but is Miego with you?"

"What do you mean 'with me'? He's not there?"

"No, he's not."

"Did he head out for something?"

Train was trying to get his head together, knowing that they had left each other hours ago and Miego was heading home. He knew him well enough to know that he wasn't checking for anybody else, so if he wasn't home with Yami, then something wasn't right.

"No, he hasn't been here since he left earlier to meet you. I waited up for him, but he didn't show up, so I went to sleep. I just woke up, and he's still not here."

"Fuck, you called him?"

"Yes, it went straight to voicemail and I haven't talked to him at all."

"Give me like an hour and I'll be there. Don't go anywhere and don't do anything. Just wait for me."

"Train, what's wrong? Did something happen tonight?"

"Nah, he's good. Don't stress. Just chill until I get there, aight?"

"Okay."

Yami ended the call and tried Miego again. Still nothing. After talking to Train, her anxiety was worse. If Train didn't know where he was, then something really had to be wrong. It wasn't like he would be laid up with another female; that wasn't his thing, so that was the least of her worries. Right now, the only thing she could think was that something had happened.

What felt like hours later, Yami pulled herself from the sofa in the living room to check the wall monitor before opening the door. She knew it was Train, but still checked just to make sure before she opened the door. Miego wasn't there, but she could still hear him in her head, and he had drilled that into her so much that it was habit. He was extremely cautious about her and Ray's safety.

"Did you find him yet?"

Train hugged Yami before he closed and locked the door or answered her question. He looked around their apartment, which was still dark since Yami hadn't bothered turning on any lights. Noticing the way he surveyed the place, she moved to the switch on the wall, and soon after, a bright glow flowed through the room.

"Not yet, but I haven't really looked yet, sis. I came straight here'

Hearing that forced a stressed look onto Yami's face as she w
over to the sofa and refilled the spot she had been in while wai

Train. Pulling her feet up and wrapping her arms around her legs, she watched Train as he followed, but stopped in front of her.

The look he wore had her even more concerned than she was before he got there. "So you haven't heard from him since he left earlier, no call, no text, nothing?"

"No, nothing since he left to go meet you, and he said he'd only be gone for a few hours. How long has it been since you've talked to him?"

"It's been a minute, but when we split, he said he was heading home—"

"That means somethings wrong, Train. He wouldn't go anywhere else," Yami said before he could finish.

"Sis, relax. You don't know that yet. Let me make a few calls and we'll figure it out. He's good, though. You have to just trust me on this one, aight?"

Train didn't know if that was true or not, but the last thing he needed was for her to be freaking out or breaking down on him. Since he didn't have a got damn clue where Miego was, it was his job to step up and make sure Yami was good in his absence.

His eyes met hers and he tried his best to wear an expression that would be convince her that everything was okay. He didn't have a clue where to even begin, but he had to do something.

Lucky for him, he didn't have to do much because his phone went off and it was a collect call.

"Bruh, what the fuck? What happened?" Train asked the second the operator finished announcing the call.

"Long story. I need you to come down here and see if you can get me out. They're on some bullshit about Kia's murder, and trying to put that shit on me. Some bitch ass detective was waiting on me when I pulled up at home. I didn't have a chance to check on Yami, so I need you to do that first and then head down here. Don't tell her shit, though."

Train's eyes moved to Yami, who was now watching him like a hawk.

"I'm here now. She called me when you didn't come home."

"Fuck. She know you're talking to me now?"

"Yep, she's right here."

"Don't tell her shit. She good, though?"

"Not really."

"Let me holla at her real quick."

Train looked up and handed the phone to Yami. "He's good, he wants to talk to you, though."

"Where are you?"

"County, just listen before you start flipping out. I'm good. Train's about to come get me, and alone. So just chill until I get there."

"No, I'm coming."

"Yamiah, no the fuck you're not. Just let Train handle it and I'll be there soon."

Yami looked at Train. "I'm not doing that. I'm going." She handed him the phone back and he shook his head.

"Yo, don't let her leave. She don't have no business down here, and I damn sure don't want her bringing Ray down here."

The situation was bad enough already, and the last thing he needed was Yami dragging Ray down there without him even knowing if they would let him go. He couldn't handle that, and he needed to focus on the issue.

"I'll do what I can, but I'm on my way. Give me a few to wrap this up."

"Hurry the fuck up. They're on some bullshit. I've been here all night, and they wouldn't even let me make a got damn call."

"I'm on it," Train said before he ended the call.

"Don't." Yami pointed her finger at Train after hearing his end of the conversation. She knew that Miego was telling him not to let her go to the police station with him, but she was going, even if she had to drive there herself.

"Don't you dare tell me to stay here. I'm going, and I don't care what he told you. So before you open your mouth to tell me different, don't bother wasting your time. I'm about to get dressed. You can try and leave me if you want, but I promise I'll drive myself, and I bet he'll be more pissed at you for letting me drive there alone than he will be for you letting me get there safely with you. So it's your choice."

Yami turned on her heels without even waiting for Train to respond. She didn't care what he was about to say because she meant what she said. After she was in her room, she quickly moved to the closet and grabbed a pair of jeans, which she stepped into before snatching a hoodie off a hanger. She stormed back into the room and headed straight to the bathroom, where she brushed her hair into a ponytail and then brushed her teeth.

She slid on a pair of no show socks and grabbed a pair of Nikes before she snatched her purse off the dresser, lifted her keys, and stormed back into the living room. Lifting her phone from the sofa, she dialed her sister while Train watched her every move. She couldn't read his expression, but she didn't really care what he was thinking. She was going.

"Yami, what's wrong?" was the first thing out of Yaz's mouth when she answered.

"I need you to come to my house and stay here with Ray."

"Why? Did something happen? Are you okay?"

"I'm fine. Miego is in jail, just come please, and hurry, Yaz."

"Shorty, what's wrong?" a male voice mumbled in the background.

"Is that Memphis?"

The second Yami said his name, Train looked right in her eyes.

"Yeah, why?"

"Nothing, just come, please. I need to go, and I can't until you get here."

"Go where, Yamiah? There's nothing you can do there with him tonight."

"Yaz, please, just come."

Yaz sighed. "Fine, we have to get dressed, but we'll be there soon."

"She coming?" Train asked as soon as Yami ended the call.

"Yeah."

"Memphis with her?"

"Yeah."

Yami waited for what she assumed would be the next question, but he didn't say or ask anything else. He just sat there watching her. She could tell he was annoyed, but she didn't care.

About an hour later, Memphis and Yaz arrived. Memphis and Train talked amongst themselves for a minute while Yami filled Yaz in on what she knew. After that, she and Train were in his car and on their way to county.

Train didn't say much, but Yami didn't care. She was processing everything that could have gone on and trying to figure out how to fix it. She was not about to lose Miego. He wasn't going to jail, that was out of the question.

"It's late, and it's likely we won't even get to see him. You know that, right?"

"Then I'll stay until I can."

"Shorty, he doesn't want you there. It was the first thing he said, and he's gonna be fucking pissed when he finds out you came. He was more worried about you being home with Ray."

"I don't care. I need to know what's going on."

"I can find out and tell you what's going on, shorty, but you being there is going to make it worse for him. He's got enough to worry about, so adding you to that mix ain't helping shit," Train said calmly. He knew the deal.

"Well, it's too late."

Train exhaled and then let it go. There was no point. For now, they were both going to the station and he'd deal with the fall out later.

Chapter Two

Miego sat silently in the interrogation room waiting for the detective to return. He had already been there for hours before they finally allowed him to make a call. Train was the first person he dialed. He damn sure wasn't about to call anyone in his family or Yami because they couldn't do shit but worry, and that wasn't about to help the situation.

When he found out that Train was already at his apartment because Yami had called him, he knew Train was gonna have a hard time leaving there without her. The only thing that would save him was the fact that she had Ray, and she was too good of a mother to drag Ray out the house at two in the morning, even if it meant coming to him.

Yami didn't need to be anywhere near this situation. He was still mad as fuck that they even arrested him for Kia's murder. They refused to tell him what they had on him, and only offered that they had an eye witness. He knew that was some bullshit because he was alone in her apartment when he shot her, and he had left out the back with no one around. The only thing that could have happened was someone seeing him enter the building, but that's not an eye witness. For all they know, he could have just been visiting.

Currently, he was tired as hell, annoyed as fuck, and ready to go home. Problem was, he didn't know how he was going to make that happen. The only plus was that it wasn't about Black or Torres, like he originally thought when they arrested him. Killing Kia, he could possibly get away with, but he knew for sure if they had any idea whatsoever that he was connected to killing Torres, they would find a way to make that shit stick.

Miego's eyes moved to the door of the interrogation room that he was in when he heard voices outside. Shortly after, the door opened and Jones entered again.

"Look, this is getting old. I'm tired, I know you're tired, and there's no way around this. Like I said, we have an eye witness who's willing to testify. Your best bet is to tell me your side, and I can see about cutting you a deal. You wait and take this to trial with your record, and that's life without parole."

Miego smiled but didn't say anything. He just watched Jones, watching him.

"Are you really that stupid that you'd rather risk life without parole instead of maybe ten to fifteen years?"

"First of all, you can't promise me shit, so don't sit here acting like you can. And I'm not risking a got damn thing because I didn't do shit. I told you, I didn't kill Kia, and I don't know who did, so why the fuck would I sit here and agree to that bullshit you're talking? The fuck outta here with that shit. Real talk. You muthafuckers think that got damn badge means something. Trust me, it don't, and I promise you this. I ain't doing time for some shit I didn't do."

"You're a real smart ass. Let's see how smart you are when the judge is sentencing you to life without parole. Like I said, we have an eye witness who's willing to testify."

"Who, muthafucker? Who the hell is your eye witness."

Jones chuckled. "Do you really think that I would tell you that so you can make them disappear?"

Miego laughed. "Yo ass watch too much TV. This ain't *Law and Order* or no shit like that. I ain't no got damn murderer, and like I said, I didn't do shit, so why the fuck would I touch your damn witness? Go find my sorry ass court appointed lawyer so they can get me the fuck outta here. Other than you telling me that he's here, I don't have shit else to say to you."

Jones sat there glaring at Miego, but he knew he couldn't do anything. He was hoping for a confession, but apparently Miego knew more than he expected him to know about his rights, so his hands were tied. For now, all he could do was wait for his lawyer to show. It was possible that he could get bail, but not likely with his record. Even so, it wouldn't happen until morning.

That would give him time to try and build a case. Jones knew that the prosecution needed more than just a simple statement from the victim's sister that she heard his voice. That was enough to get the warrant for his arrest, but only because he called in a favor. The prosecution would need more, and they had already gone through the apartment, canvassed the neighborhood, and hadn't found a damn thing. So if he couldn't secure a confession, it was likely Miego was going to walk.

"Jones, lawyer is here."

Looking at Miego, Jones frowned and then walked out the door. He left just as a tall, thin, nerdy looking guy with glasses entered and shut the door behind him.

"Mr. Grant." He extended a hand to Miego. "I'm Jason Taylor. I'll be representing you."

"Can you get me out of here?"

"Not tonight, but possibly in the morning once you're arraigned."

"Fuck. What do they have?"

Taylor was looking down at some papers he had placed on the table in front of him.

"Do you know a Lena Johnson?"

"Yeah, that's Kia's sister, why?"

"Says here, she gave a signed statement that she was on the phone with her sister when you arrived. She heard her sister say your name and then she heard your voice. Is that true? They pulled the cellphone records showing that she was on the phone with her sister at the time of the incident. Were you with her, the victim?"

Miego thought for a minute. He remembered that Kia was on the phone, but he also knew that he didn't speak until after the call was disconnected, so Lena lied."

"Nah, I wasn't there, so there's no got damn way she heard my voice. That's all they have?"

"Looks like it, which means that with no other evidence, it's likely the prosecution can't build a case."

"Then get me the fuck outta here."

"I will try first thing in the morning, but can you account for your whereabouts that evening?"

Miego considered it, but he wasn't about to put Yami in the middle of any of this. He'd have to do it without her. She had Ray to think about."

"I was with a friend, but I'd rather not say who. I'll take my chances with what they don't have. I mean, you said they don't have a case, right?"

"True, but something as simple as an alibi could end all this right now, and I can definitely get you out of here in the morning. Just think about it."

"Yeah, aight. So what now?"

"They process you, you get arraigned in the morning, and we request bail. In the meantime, I'll try to get the case thrown out due to lack of evidence. They really don't have anything to build a case with, to be honest. I'm going to speak to the arresting officer. Looks like he's the one who secured the warrant. Have you been treated fairly since you've been here?"

"The fuck you think? I'm sitting here handcuffed to a got damn table. How fucking fair is that? For some shit I didn't do."

Taylor chuckled. "I see you point. Give me a minute and I'll be right back. But you have two visitors. I can probably get them in to see you if you would like."

"Two?"

"Yes. A gentleman and a young lady."

Miego instantly got heated, knowing that Yami was there."

"Yeah, 'preciate that."

Taylor nodded and left the room. A few minutes later, the door opened again, and in walked Train and Yami. She looked relieved to see his face, if only for a minute, until she realized he was upset.

"Yo, why are you here? And where the fuck is Ray?"

"Home, with Yaz."

Miego glanced at Train, who held his hands up. "She wouldn't listen, bruh. I told her what you said."

Train leaned against the wall while Yami pulled her chair around to Miego and sat down. She placed her hands in her lap and just stared at him.

"You hard headed as fuck, shorty. I really don't want you caught up in any of this," Miego said, placing his hand on her thigh. He didn't want her there, but couldn't help but be happy that she was near him. She was his calm in a sea of chaos.

"I told you I had you, so if it means being here, then I'm here. What's it about, anyway?"

"It's not important," was all Miego said.

"It is important if you're here. So don't do that. It's too late to try and hide it. So just tell me."

Miego glanced at the window and then at Train. "Somebody killed Kia," Miego said calmly, to see how Yami would react.

She was with him the night it happened, so she already knew that. He was testing her to see if she knew what to say and what not to say. It could cost him, but for some reason he had faith in her.

"Well, you didn't do it because you were with me. And I'll tell them that."

He chuckled. "I didn't say when."

"Doesn't matter, you're always with me," she said and shrugged.

"True, but stay out of it. I'll figure it out. This is the last thing you need. Just worry about Ray. You know how to get in the safe if you need anything, and Train's got you for anything else."

"But if you were with me, then..."

"Yamiah, no, let it go," Miego said firmly, just as the door opened and Taylor walked back in.

"Okay, we're all set. You'll be arraigned in the morning and I'll be there. So you're here for now, and they'll take you to the courthouse in the morning.

"What if he had an alibi?" Yami asked, cutting her eyes at Miego before turning to Taylor, in order to avoid the nasty look that she knew Miego was about to return.

"Doesn't matter, because I don't," he said, cutting his eyes at her and then Taylor.

"Is this the friend that you were with?" Taylor asked.

"Yes."

"No."

Miego and Yami answered at the same time, causing Train to chuckle as he stood across the room watching. Miego was bound and determined to keep Yamiah out of it, while she was trying her best to be sitting right in the middle of it.

"She's not my alibi," Miego said again, but this time with a little more aggression.

"I know that you want to protect her, but with her statement, I can guarantee that we can get this thrown out before it even becomes a case.

"Nah, we're good. I'll take my chances."

"Can I give a statement without his permission?" Yami asked, totally ignoring Miego.

Her question caused Train to chuckle again, which made Miego send visual daggers across the room at him.

"Uhhm yeah, you can," Taylor answered, also ignoring Miego and focusing on Yami.

"Let's do it then."

"Yamiah, don't do that shit, just let it go."

"You can be mad all you want, but I'm not about to let you sit here for something we both know you didn't do. Especially not if I can do something about it."

She looked at him so serious like she actually believed what she was saying, even though she knew good and damn well that he was guilty. She didn't care though, if it meant that she could get him out of it, then she was going to say whatever she had to.

"Fuck. Come on, shorty, can you please let this go?" Miego pleaded.

Yami stood, leaned over him, kissed his lips, and then the side of his face, before whispering against his ear, "If you got me, then I got you. I'm doing this, and you can't change my mind, so please stop trying and just let me help."

She let her lips touch the side of his face one last time before she looked right at Taylor. "Please take my statement."

Knowing that he wasn't about to change her mind, Miego let it go. Yami followed Taylor to the door, and just before they left, he looked across the room.

"Yo, go with her."

Miego motioned to Train, who nodded and left with them. As much as he was trying to keep her safe, she was doing the same for him. And as pissed as he was about it, he had to respect her for that.

Chapter Three

"How much longer?" Yami asked as her eyes fell on Taylor.

He had managed to get the case thrown out due to lack of evidence combined with her statement, so they were currently waiting for Miego to be processed to go home.

"Shouldn't be long. They're finishing up his paperwork right now," Taylor said, feeling pleased about the work he had done.

Yami stood and started pacing again. She had been alternating between sitting and pacing for the past half hour as they waited for Miego to be processed.

"Yo, shorty, you making me dizzy as fuck. Can you please sit down?" Train asked, looking up at her from his phone.

Train had been with her for damn near the past twelve hours and she was grateful. He kept her mind off what was going on with Miego, and being around him so much the last day had made her realize that he was a lot like Miego. Not as rude, but he was close to it, and he had truly looked out for her the entire time. He made sure she ate, kept her busy so that she didn't think too much, and checked in with Memphis and Yaz, who had Ray, so she could focus on what was going on with Miego.

Train had stepped up and was the big brother to her.

"Shut up. Just ignore me." Yami rolled her eyes at him.

"How the fuck and I supposed to do that when you're walking right here in front of me, Yamiah? Damn, sit your little ass down, shorty. I swear they need to hurry this shit up." His eyes were still on his phone, but he wore a smirk, so she knew that he was only playing with her.

"Why you pacing like that, shorty? This shit is over with now."

Hearing that voice made her heart race. When she looked up and saw him moving toward her, she took off and jumped on him, throwing her arms around his neck and her legs around his waist. He held her in place with his arms while her lips crashed against his.

"So you're happy to see me on this side, shorty?" Miego asked with a grin.

Her arms tightened around his neck before she pressed her face against his. "Let's go home, and I'll show you how much," she said only loud enough for him to hear.

"Man, get your horny ass down and let me talk to dude." Miego kissed her neck and held her against his chest for a few more seconds before he finally allowed her body to slide down his so that she was standing again.

Train was on his feet and met him with a pound and then a hug. "My nigga. I was thinking I was gon' have to blow this bitch up to get you out."

"Shit, I was hoping you would. I damn sure wasn't about to be in that cage again. Fuck what you heard."

Train laughed. "Nah, not even. Bonnie over here was gon' get you out one way or another." Train lowered his arm around Yamiah's shoulder and pulled her into his side. He didn't see it coming, but Yamiah had proven her loyalty. She was just what Miego needed, and you couldn't put a price on that.

"Yo, so what now?" Miego asked, addressing Taylor.

"For now, there's no case. Unless they find more evidence, you're good. You haven't been proven innocent, so there is always a possibility, but the case was thrown out for lack of evidence. There's a difference."

"So they could come after him again?" Yami asked with her face balled up. She hadn't really thought about that, and didn't really know much about law.

"Yes, there's always the possibility, but it's not likely. After seeing what they had and talking to a few people, I'm pretty sure this is it," Taylor said.

Miego extended his hand to Taylor and the two men shook.

"I appreciate what you did to get this taken care of."

"Just doing my job." He reached in his pocket and pulled out a card. "I'm branching off on my own. If you ever need anything, call me. I'd be glad to help you out."

Miego chuckled. "Aight, I'll do that. But, bruh, I plan on making this the last time I see the inside of a courtroom or a muthafucking jail."

"Can't say I blame you. Good luck, though, and I'm here if you need me."

Taylor walked over and lifted his briefcase from the bench that they had sat on while waiting for Miego to get processed out of the system, and then he left.

"See, shorty? Calm the fuck down. I'm good, now let's go home."

"Aye, let me holla at you real quick." Train glanced at Yami, who nodded and stepped back to give them some privacy.

She pulled out her phone to check in with Yaz, who had stayed with Ray and then got her up and off to daycare. Yami had skipped classes for the day to be there with Miego, and now all she had to do was get him home and pick up Ray from daycare later.

Miego watched Yami while he listened to Train. He was grateful that she had come through for him, even though he wasn't pleased about it. Either way, it was done, so there wasn't anything that he could do about it.

"So, no word yet on the fire or the bodies?"

"They announced on the news that they found both of them dead, but no leads. The only thing they said was that it appeared to be a drug deal, but they're still working on it. Far as I can tell, we're in the clear. They showed the warehouse on the news and the entire thing had burned to the ground, nothing left, which means that there's nothing left that can connect any of us."

"Hopefully, we're done with that shit. I can't take another situation. Not right now. Fuck, she still doesn't know, does she?" Again, his eyes fell on Yami, who looked up at the same time and smiled at him.

"Nah, I didn't say shit 'cause it wasn't my place. Besides, I didn't know how you wanted to handle it."

"I'll tell her. It's more about Ray than her. She don't understand shit like that."

"True, but she's young as hell, and she got you, with your Mr. Mom ass. She's good, yo." Train laughed, thinking about how Miego was with Ray. She was damn near his kid already.

"You're right, she's good. But I'm ready to get the fuck outta here. She's got the car, right?"

"Yeah, she made me take her to get it. She was dead set on bringing your ass home, bruh. You got one right there." Train pointed to Yami, who wasn't paying attention to either of them.

"She aight," Miego confessed, but he knew she was a keeper.

There was no doubt in his mind that Yami was down for him, and he was going to make it his mission to be that for her.

Yami ended her call with her sister and walked over to Miego. She moved her body right next to his so that she was positioned at his side, with an arm around his waist. Naturally, his arm fell around her shoulder and he moved her closer to him.

"Damn, sis, it's like that? Soon as his punk ass is free, you put me down." Train pretended to be offended.

"You know it's all love, but I missed my man."

"Fuck him. You don't have to explain shit to his ass," Miego said.

"Damn, that's fucked up, bruh." Train shook his head and chuckled, which made Miego laugh.

"I'm just fucking with you. You know I appreciate that shit, but on the real, let's get the fuck outta here. I need a shower and some pussy.

"Miego." Yami yelled like she was actually surprised.

"What? Shit, I mean it, so don't look at me like that. In fact, let's roll so you can get me right."

"Yo, I'm out. I'll let y'all have that shit." Train grabbed Yami's arms and pulled her into a hug. After he released her, he dapped Miego. "I'll check in with you later, but for now, I'm 'bout to take my ass home and crawl the up under the fucking bed. I feel like I was the one in the cage."

The three of them laughed as they headed out the court house. The second Miego and Yami reached their apartment, he stripped out of his clothes and went straight for the shower. He had never been so happy to be home in all his life. Every other time he had been locked up, it wasn't like he had much to miss. Not saying that his freedom wasn't important, but this time, knowing that he was leaving Yami and Ray had his head all fucked up. The entire time he was there, that was the one thing that bothered him the most.

Having the thought so strong made him laugh to himself. He knew what it meant, even if he wasn't going to say it out loud or admit it. Yami had his heart, and he didn't know what to do with that.

"You feel like sharing?"

Her small voice snapped him out of his head. When she pulled the glass door to join him, his eyes moved across her body, instantly causing a reaction in his. He was about to make up for lost time, and from the look in her eyes, she was thinking the same thing.

****

Miego was stretched out on the sofa with Yami on top of him. His hand moved across her back while the other was folded behind his head. She had been quiet for a while, and her breathing had slowed down to a steady pace, so he knew that she was on the verge of falling asleep. After the way he had just put it down, he understood why.

Yami had begged for mercy, which he refused to give. It had only been one night away from her, but he felt like he needed to make up for lost time. Not only for himself, but for her too. Now, here she was, damn near passed out, refusing to move.

"Shorty, I need to talk to you about something." He lifted his hand and moved her hair out of her face, while looking down at her. Her eyes were closed and they didn't open even after he spoke.

"Yamiah, you hear me?" This time, he sat up and pulled her with him. She didn't have a choice but to pay attention to him.

She leaned back against the arm of the sofa while she adjusted her body so that she was comfortable against him again. Now she was positioned between his legs with her shoulder against his chest and his arms around her.

"Okay, I'm listening." She yawned and then let her head fall back a little.

"I need to tell you something, but I don't want you to flip out on me."

She looked up at him with concern in her eyes for a second before she sat up completely. He thought about holding her in place, but decided against it and let her go. She was still positioned between his legs, but was now sitting up.

"Is something wrong?" she asked, not really prepared to deal with any more issues. The past day had been enough to last her for a while, as far as she was concerned.

"Not really. Well, not for me anyway, but it might be for you."

"Miego, don't do that, just tell me."

"It's about Black."

Now she was really worried. The last thing she wanted or needed was for Miego to have issues with him. "Did he do something?"

Miego chuckled. "Nah, but I did. Let's just say you won't have to worry about him anymore?"

Yami knew what that meant, but she had to ask anyway. "Is he dead?"

"Yeah."

"When?"

"It don't matter."

She sat there for a minute processing. It wasn't like she didn't care, she did. How could she not? They shared a child and she wasn't heartless, but after everything he had done to her and put her through, she just couldn't find the energy to be upset about it. In fact, the only thing that had her feeling any emotions at all about it was her daughter and Simone. She knew they both loved him, even if she didn't anymore. Ray had lost her father while Simone had lost her son.

"Yamiah, you good, shorty?"

She shrugged. "Is it bad that I don't really have any feelings about it? I mean, it's Ray's father, and I know she loved him, but that's it. I can be sad for her, but I don't really have any other feelings about it. Well, other than his mother. No matter how bad he was, it was still her son, and I can't imagine losing Ray, so I know it's going to hurt when she finds out. I have to talk her."

"Not now, not until shit calms down. And no, it's not bad that you don't have feelings about it. Considering everything that he did to you, you have the right to distance yourself from feeling anything about it, or him. It doesn't make you a bad person, it makes you human."

She nodded and he pulled her back against his body. "It's fucked up and I know it. But I promise you this, you and Ray were more important to me than that muthafucker, so I don't have no regrets, but

I don't want you to have any either. I can live with the choices that I make, but I can't expect you to, so feel how you need to, shorty. I promise, I'm good with that, but just know that I got you and Ray, for whatever that means. I meant it the first time I said it, and I mean it now, so don't ever question that. If it means killing the whole got damn city to make sure you're good, then trust me, shorty. I'll do that shit and won't give it a second thought."

Yami laughed, not really knowing why, but hearing him talk like that had her convinced. She was already feeling it, but day by day he was proving it.

"The fuck you laughing for?" Miego said, peering down at her.

"Careful, I might start to think you're catching feelings," she said, holding her head back so she could look at him.

Unable to hide the smile that formed, he kissed her and then laughed. "The fuck outta here with that. I just feel sorry for your ass. Ain't nobody catching feelings, shorty. It takes more than good head to make that shit happen."

"Oh my God. You are so damn insensitive. Did you really have to ruin the moment?" She rolled her eyes and tried to pull away from him, but he laughed, while he tightened his hold on her.

"Chill, I'm just fucking with you. You're such a got damn cry baby, shorty. For real, though. Let's go get my baby girl. I miss her."

Before he let her go, he kissed her a few more times and then the two got up and prepared to leave. Like it or not, he had a family, and he was going to protect them with his life.

Chapter Four

Yami pulled her backpack up over her shoulder as she moved to her car. She wasn't paying attention to the people moving around her because she was in the process of sending a text, so when Lena walked up to her and grabbed her arm, it scared the shit out of her.

"You need to tell the truth. I don't know how you can live with yourself, protecting him like that."

Yami snatched away from her grasp and squared up, not really knowing what to expect. She recognized Lena from Miego's arraignment hearing, but she didn't know her.

"I'm not protecting anyone, and I don't know what you're talking about. But if you put your damn hands on me again, you're going to need protection from me."

Lena laughed sarcastically. "Bitch, please. I wish you would try to come at me like that, but this ain't even about that. I just wanted to tell you that this ain't over, I promise you that. Miego killed my sister, and I'll figure out a way to prove it. Since you call yourself being stupid enough to support a murderer, I guess that means I'm coming for you too."

"Do what you want, but there's nothing to prove. He was with me that night, and that isn't going to change, so good luck with that."

"Yeah, well maybe you're the one who pulled the trigger. Maybe I'll just put that bug in somebody's ear," Lena said with a smirk.

Her eyes moved up and down Yami's body before she sucked her teeth. "Trust me, this ain't over," she said before she walked off.

Yami watched her for a minute before she unlocked her car and got in. It bothered her a little, but she knew that there wasn't really anything Lena could do to prove that either she or Miego had killed Kia. There was no evidence, and Taylor had already called to tell them that the cops had basically given up trying. Either way, she didn't like her coming at her like that, so she called Miego to let him know what had just happened.

"Hold up, shorty... Yo, stop fucking cheating. How you gon' keep the game going when I told you to pause that shit so I can answer my phone."

She then heard Train's voice in the background.

"Shit, I told your ass no, but I was winning before that shit."

"What the fuck ever, what's up shorty?"

"I just saw Kia's sister."

"The fuck you mean saw her?" Now she had his full attention. He dropped his control and stood, folding one arm across his chest while holding the phone in place with the other.

Train's eyes were on him as he dropped his control and stood a few feet away from him.

"I was leaving campus and she just showed up. She grabbed my arm, talking about this is not over. She said that she's going to go to the cops and tell them that maybe I was the one who shot her sister, since I was protecting you."

"The fuck she mean protecting me? You told the truth," Miego said, knowing that they were on the phone and not wanting to take any chances. He looked up at Train before he continued. "Look, just chill for a minute and I'll come meet you. Where you at?"

"No, I'm fine. Don't do that. We can talk when I get home. I have to go get Ray and then meet Simone."

"Yamiah, just let me come meet you. You can do that shit another time."

"Miego, I'm good. I was just calling to tell you, but we can talk later, okay."

"Yeah, aight, text me when you get there and before you leave."

"I will."

They ended the call and Yamiah shot Simone a quick text to let her know that she was on her way.

Miego, on the other hand, slid his phone back in his pocket and looked right at Train.,

"What's up, something going on with sis?"

"Lena's dumb ass showed up at her school talking shit about going to the cops to tell them that Yamiah was the one who shot Kia.

Train waved him off, not worried about Lena going to the cops, but he wasn't feeling the fact that Lena ran up on her like that. Just like Miego, Yamiah was now his family too, and a problem for her was a problem for him. "They ain't gon' do shit about that. First, she claims that she heard your voice, and then she goes back to say shorty did it. They still don't have shit, so they can't do shit anyway. Taylor already cleared you on that."

"True, but she needs to stay in her fucking lane. Ain't gon' be too many more times with the running up on my shorty like that without it being an issue."

"Look, yo, I know you're not feeling that shit, but you can't make that move. She come up missing and they'll damn sure rethink that shit."

"Yeah, you're right, especially if anybody saw that shit that just went down with her and Yamiah. But if she keeps playing, I'm gon' have a conversation with her."

Train laughed. "Nah, muthafucker, I'll have a conversation with her. I can't trust your ass. You'll fuck around and choke the shit outta her dumb ass and we'll be right back to square one. We got money to make, and you got a family to raise. Stay the fuck away from Lena, and I mean that shit, Miego."

He looked at Train with a straight face, not breaking until Train spoke again. "Yo, I'm serious as fuck right now, so whatever is in your head, shut that shit down. Right muthafucking now." Train didn't bother waiting for a reaction, he just walked to his bar and pulled the door to the mini fridge. After he had two beers in his hand, he passed one off to Miego, who took it and sat back down on the sofa.

His mind was still working, but he knew Train was right. For now, he was letting it go.

"It's been almost two weeks, and still nothing about Torres or Black, so I'm guessing we're good on that." Train lifted the control and restarted the game.

"Yeah, I hear Bank took over his shit."

"Yep, just kept it moving like nothing ever happened," Train said.

"That's some fucked up shit. I bet he was glad we killed Black." Miego chuckled as he thought about it. Word on the street was that none of Black's people really liked him, they were either scared of him or just tolerated him. "Yo, if some shit went down with me like that, I expect your ass to take some time off and mourn for me. Don't just act like I never existed."

Train turned toward Miego and looked at him like he was crazy. "The fuck, man? You family. I know you know better than that."

The intense look that Train wore really made Miego laugh. Train looked like he wanted to hit him. "Bruh, I'm just saying. Why the fuck you look like you want to rock the shit out of me?"

"Cause your dumb ass saying bullshit like that. I ought to shoot you my damn self. The fuck outta here with all that you better mourn me. First of all, you ain't going nowhere, and second of all, that shit is already understood. Now pick up your damn control so I can beat your ass on this damn game. Done pissed me the fuck off."

Miego just chuckled. If he didn't know anything else in life to be true, he knew that Train was always down for him. That wasn't changing. They both had proven their loyalty enough times to know that it was a non-factor.

****

"Thank you for coming," Simone said over her shoulder as she escorted Yami and Ray into her kitchen.

It had been a week since the funeral for her son, and two weeks since she found out about his death. She was still an emotional wreck, but she was managing. Regardless of who he was, he was still her son, and she loved him. So knowing that he was gone was hard.

"You don't have to thank me for coming. I told you it doesn't matter what he and I had, you're family and you're always going to be."

All of a sudden, Yami felt sad for her role in Simone losing her son. Even though Black came after Miego and it was personal, when it was all said and done, he killed Black because of her.

"I appreciate that, sweetheart. I just wish he had been a better man to you."

"Grandma, can I have cookies?" Ray asked, causing their attention to move to her as she climbed into one of the kitchen chairs and placed her iPad down on the table.

"You sure can. What kind, sweetheart."

"Chocolate chip. Mommy, do you want cookies too?" Ray asked, grinning at her mother.

"No, you can have them. I'm going to talk to grandma while you eat them."

Yami walked over and kissed her daughter on the cheek before smoothing back the edges of her hair. Simone placed a plate that had three oversized freshly baked cookies in front of Ray along with a plastic cup filled with milk.

"Here you go."

"Thank you," Ray said before lifting one and shoving it into her mouth to take a bite that almost equaled half the cookie. Yami looked at Simone and frowned, but she shrugged and smiled.

"Moms set the rules and grandmas break them," was all she said as she and Yami moved to the other side of the kitchen to talk privately.

"Her birthday is in a few weeks. I'd like to be there for whatever you do," Simone said, looking over at her granddaughter and then back to Yami. Ray was all she had left of her son, and that made her sad.

"Of course. You know I wouldn't do anything without you there," Yami said truthfully. She loved Simone and had no plans to change her relationship with Ray.

"Can I ask you something?" Simone's expression grew serious and her eyes seemed to get sad.

"Sure."

Simone swallowed hard and then looked Yami right in her eyes. "Do you know who did it?"

Yami felt like her heart stopped, but she kept her cool, returned a confident stare, and answered with a simple, "No."

Simone didn't speak for a minute, but Yami could tell from the look in Simone's eyes that she didn't believe her.

"They asked... the cops..." She paused for a minute. "They kept questioning me about Marshall's life and his enemies. Was there anyone who would try to harm him? They asked me about you and the relationship you had. I told them you would never hurt Marshall, that he had hurt you plenty of times, but that you would never hurt him. He was my son, but that didn't excuse the things he did. I just want you to know that I'm glad you're free. As horrible as that may be, I just want you to be happy, and I love you no matter what."

"Thank you. I know that he's your son and—"

"Yamiah, don't do that. Marshall did this to himself. I blame him, well him and his father."

With sad eyes, Yami looked around. She had been there several times and realized she had yet to see Nigel. They didn't communicate much. In fact, she always felt like he didn't care for her, but he had always been civil.

"How is he?" Yami asked, curious about how he was taking it.

Simone's expression grew sad before she spoke again. "He's not taking it well. In fact, he moved out. Said he needed space and time, to think. Apparently, me making peace with it, didn't sit too well with him." Simone slumped her shoulders a bit. "I don't know what else to do. It hurts my heart. I loved my son, but holding hate in my heart won't change who he was or the fact that he's not coming back. I guess that makes me a monster, according to Nigel. I can't let that weigh on me, and you can't either."

Not really knowing what to say, Yiam just nodded before Simone wrapped her arms around her. She hugged her back, and for the first time since she found out about Black, she cried. Nothing major, she just had a moment of weakness. More for Simone than for him, but after today, she was never going to worry about him again. She knew that Simone was telling her that it was okay to let go and move on, and that was exactly what she was going to do.

She and Ray stayed and talked with Simone for a few more hours before she decided to head home. Not wanting Miego to worry, she sent him a text to let him know that she was on her way, and he let her know that he was there waiting.

When she got home, she found Miego in the living room on the sofa with the remote in one hand, looking like he had just woke up. Ray ran right to him and jumped in his lap.

She held up a Ziploc bag, almost hitting him in the face with it because she held it so close,

"I brought you cookies. My grandma made them," Ray said, holding up her gift for Miego, which made him laugh. This little girl had his heart and everything else about him wrapped around her little finger.

"Word. You thought about me, baby girl?"

"Yep, can I have one of yours?" she asked, smiling from ear to ear.

"Ray, no. You can't give someone a present and then ask them for it back."

"Mommy, I'm not. I didn't ask for it back, I asked him to share."

Yami rolled her eyes and Miego laughed before he kissed Ray on the forehead. "You're good, baby girl. You can have one, but only one, and put mine on the counter."

"Thank you." She pecked him on the cheek before hopping down out of his lap.

Yami walked over and sat down next to him. His hand instantly went to her thigh, giving it a gentle squeeze before she lifted his hand and intertwined their fingers.

They both watched Ray lift the plastic bowl off the counter and then drop her cookie in it before she planted herself on the floor in the living room. Miego lifted the remote with his free hand and turned to Disney Channel for her, already knowing she was about to ask.

"How'd it go?" he asked, not really wanting to have a discussion about Black or his mother. But if it affected Yami and Ray, then he made it his business to be involved.

"It was good. Kind of weird, though. It was like she was giving me her blessing to move on. I mean she had already done that, but with everything going on, it was different this time."

"People know their kids. She knew who her son was, and maybe she was at peace with the fact that she loved him, but you didn't have to. Long as it's not a problem, then it's all good."

"She said the cops asked about me, about my relationship with him. She asked if I knew who did it."

That got Miego's attention, but he remained calm. He wasn't worried about Yamiah saying anything, but he was curious about what the cops knew.

"Oh yeah? What did she tell them?"

"That I wouldn't hurt him, and that he hurt me. I told her I didn't know who did it."

Miego lifted her hand and kissed the back of it. He was conflicted about everything. He didn't really care about how things worked out for him, but he didn't like the fact that Yami had to lie about it.

"I hate putting that on you. That's why I don't want you connected to the things I do."

"You didn't put that on me, so let it go. I have, and you need to." She lifted her body and straddled his lap, connecting her lips to his and then looking into his eyes.

"I'm glad you're in my life, and I accept everything that comes with that. It's my choice, so don't ever feel like you're forcing anything on me, okay?"

Miego chuckled and then kissed her again, but didn't say anything.

"What?" Yami asked with a frown.

"Nothing, man."

"Then why you looking at me like that?"

He kissed the tip of her nose. "It's nothing."

He looked over at Ray, who was in her own world, laughing about something she was watching and then back at Yamiah. He didn't need to tell her that she and Ray were everything to him. He would kill for them, die for them, and everything in between. Yamiah would learn that over time, so for now, it didn't need to be explained.

Chapter Five

"Yazmine, you keep saying the same shit, but then you do something completely different. You either in this or you're not. I don't have time to be playing fucking games, shorty. We ain't kids."

"Why is it playing games just because I'm not sure?" Yaz snapped, looking across at Memphis as he drove them to Train's apartment to meet Yami and Miego for dinner. It was a couples thing, and Train even planned to have Lisa there for the first time, making the circle complete.

"What the fuck is there to be unsure about? We been kicking it strong as hell. I ain't fucking with nobody else and yo ass better not be either. Shit, Yaz, what else is there? We act like a got damn couple, so why the hell you keep throwing that shit out there like we ain't? How you gon' tell my sister we just chillin'? We doing more than just chilling if I'm in your bed almost every night, and I'm the only one you fucking. I'm damn near paying all your bills, and if you need anything, it's my phone you hitting. Fuck that bullshit you talking, this ain't chillin' shorty, I'm yours and you're mine."

Yaz opened her mouth to say something, but didn't know what. He was right, they may as well be a couple, but she had learned that titles were like a green light to fuck up. That was how things worked with Trez. The second they made things official was when the hoes started showing up. She knew that she was wrong for penalizing Memphis for Trez and his fuck ups, but it was hard not to.

Things were good the way they were, and it was like her safety net. Yami kept telling her that she was going to lose him if she kept trying to pretend like what they had didn't mean anything, but she felt like she'd lose him if she did stop. If he felt like he had her and got comfortable with that, then he might feel like he could also have someone else too. Men had a way of making you feel secure, just so you wouldn't think it was possible for them to cheat.

"What? You don't have shit to say to that?" Memphis asked after he parked in front of Train's spot.

"Can we just talk about it later?" Yaz asked, holding the handle to the door.

"For what? So you can hit me with the same bullshit again? Just forget it, yo. Let's go so we can get this shit over with. I need a got damn drink, fucking with your indecisive ass." Memphis opened the door to get out, and then waited on the sidewalk for Yaz.

After he locked his car doors, he waited for her to lead the way, but kept his distance. He was pissed with her, but still going to make sure she was safe. Memphis always walked behind Yaz, just enough to peep his surroundings and keep an eye on her to make sure she was good.

When they got to the door, Yaz rang the bell, and a few moments later, Train opened the door with his son in his arms. He hugged Yaz and dapped Memphis, but noticed neither of them looked happy.

"The fuck wrong with y'all?" he asked after they were inside with the door shut.

"Man, don't ask, just point me to something strong. I need that shit," Memphis said, waving Train off.

"What up, fam?" Miego said as soon as Memphis was in the room. He dapped him and pulled him into a hug.

"Yo, give him a damn drink. Yaz done pissed him off about something."

Miego chuckled as he moved to the bar. "Man, I told you 'bout fucking with her. The fuck she do? Running her damn mouth, I bet," Miego said while pouring Memphis a shot of vodka, which he accepted and downed before he nodded for another.

"Man, chill with that shit. But, nah, it ain't that. She so fucking insecure. I swear on everything, I'm trying to do the right thing, but she on that we just chilling shit. I'm like, nah shorty, if I'm in your shit every night and paying your bills, ain't no damn chillin'. We in this shit."

Train laughed. "Damn, bruh, you sound mad as fuck. It's like that? Why you don't think she trust you. You slipped?"

"Hell no, I mean I fucked around a little in the beginning, but that was before we were solid. I don't have time to be juggling females and shit. That's played, but on the real, dude she was with before did her dirty, and she's acting like that's gon' be me. I ain't no got damn cheater."

Miego handed him another shot and he downed that one too. "I feel you on that, bruh, I ain't got time for that shit either. I'm all about my money, so fuck keeping up with a bunch of ungrateful hoes that only wanna spend that shit. That shit is played like a muthafucker. If I can't get what I need from Yamiah's little ass then that means she ain't the one, and trust me when I say, she's holding me down. On some real shit."

"Your whipped ass." Train laughed.

"Fuck yeah. It's diseases and shit out there. I'm not risking my shit falling off. You on your own with that. I keep telling you to grow the fuck up and do right by Lisa, or the next man will."

"Man, she's good," Train said.

"Fuck all that. I'm good with Yaz, but she better figure that shit out, and she better do that shit fast, or I promise I'm done."

"Figure what out?" Yami asked when she entered the room. She walked up to Memphis and hugged him and then reached for Tavion. "Lisa said to bring him to her so that she can feed him, and you and my sister must be fighting 'cause she sitting in the corner with her lips poked out."

Memphis chuckled at the thought of Yaz pouting. He could see her face in his head, and it made him smile, but only for a minute.

"You better talk to her. She don't know that the fuck she wants, and she better figure it out before I make the decision for her," Memphis said.

"You are what she wants. You already know that," Yami said with a frown.

"What the fuck ever, I damn sure can't tell. Let her tell it we're chilling. If we chilling, then she shouldn't mind if I chill with somebody else too."

"Memphis, don't say that."

"Talk to her, Yami. I'm over this shit."

Yami stared at him for a minute before she kissed the top of Tavion's head. "I will." She walked over to Miego to steal a kiss also, but he mushed her.

"Man, gon' with that. You see me with my people. Trying to punk me and shit."

"So kissing me is punking you? Okay, remember that." She turned to walk away, but he followed her and bear hugged her before she could leave the room.

"Chill, with your bratty ass. I swear you're a fucking baby sometimes." He planted kisses on her neck and then her cheek before she shrugged him off and left the room smiling and satisfied. He always called her a baby, but he made sure to give her exactly what she wanted, every time, without hesitation.

When Yami was back in the room with the girls, she planted several kisses all over Tavion before she handed him off to Lisa. She had been around Train's son a few times, but this was her first time being around Lisa. Train never really had her around, which Yami couldn't really figure out why. Lisa was pretty and she seemed chill, which made Yami believe that it was more about the fact that Train was always up to something, and he didn't want her close to Lisa.

His life was his business, so Yami would never get in the middle of that. It wasn't her thing.

"Hey, fat boy," Lisa said, smiling as she took her son into her arms. He was adorable, but other than his eyes and square face, he looked just like Lisa.

"He's a good baby, he never cries," Yami said, smiling at Lisa dealing with Tavion and remembering Ray as a baby.

Ray had cried about everything, all the time, and not little cries, loud piercing screams that had you questioning your sanity. Watching Tavion, Yami was thinking that she might be willing to try it again because he was such a good baby.

"He is. I swear, sometimes he's so mellow I worry about him. It's kind of crazy, but I guess it's a good thing."

"Nothing like Ray, her little ass used to holler about everything." Yaz looked across the room at her niece who was sitting at a table coloring.

"Really?" Lisa asked, propping her son up in her lap while he held his bottle.

"Oh my God, yes. She was such a cry baby. It drove me crazy."

"Then I'm really glad he's not like that. I don't think I would have the patience for it."

"You have no idea. Such a brat," Yaz added.

"I'm not a cry baby," Ray yelled from across the room and slammed her tiny fist filled crayons down on the table in front of her.

Yaz and Yami both looked at each other and laughed before Yami made her way to her daughter. She leaned down and kissed her on the side of her face before pressing hers against it.

"Not now, Ray, but you used to cry all the time when you were a baby."

"But I don't anymore." Ray pouted.

"No, you don't. You're a big girl and Mommy loves you."

Yami kissed her daughter's face again and Yaz laughed at how spoiled her niece was because just like that, she was over it and coloring again. Yami made her way back to the girls with her hand on her hip, peering at her sister.

"Speaking of brats, what's going on with you and Memphis?"

"How the hell does that make you think about me and Memphis?"

Yami laughed as Lisa and Yaz waited. "Hell, it doesn't, but I needed to just throw that out there, so spill."

"You're slow as hell, Yamiah, and there's nothing to spill."

"Girl, whatever. If there's nothing to spill then why is he in there looking mad at the world and threatening me to talk to you. What am I supposed to be talking to you about, Yazmine?" Yami pointed at her sister and waited.

"Nothing, he's just in his feelings because I said we weren't in a relationship and that we were just chilling."

"Chillin'?" Yami cocked her head to the side and looked at her sister like she was crazy. "So he be in your bed almost every night, he's paying your bills, and y'all damn near live together. If that's chillin' then what the hell is a relationship? Please break that down for me, Yaz."

"Wait, so you guys are tight like that, but you not claiming him? Why not?" Lisa asked, deciding to weigh in.

"Because it's still new, and there's no point of rushing things. We're good like we are." Yaz shrugged.

"You sound stupid, Yazmine. Don't make him pay because Trez was a dick. Memphis is not Trez, and he's already proven that to you.

Hell, he's fighting for your dumb ass while you're fighting against him. How much more can you ask for?"

"Exactly, you see what I'm dealing with? Train is screwing everything moving, even though he claims he's not. I'm not stupid. I'm trying to be patient because I love him and I don't want my son to have a stepmoms and dads. If you have a man that's trying to be committed to you, then you better jump on it."

"See, that's the thing. Just because he wants to put a label on it, doesn't mean that he's going to be faithful. It just means he wants me comfortable enough to think that he will be. That's when all the shit starts. But if we keep things like they are, then he'll always be wondering if I'll just walk, which means he'll be more cautious about the choices he makes."

Yami and Lisa both looked at Yaz for a minute before their eyes fell on each other and they laughed.

"Girl, you need to rethink that plan. A man will cheat if he wants to cheat. Title or not. I'm living proof of that. You either trust him or you don't, and if you don't, then don't be with him. But that game you're playing is only going to make him walk away, if he's really serious about locking things down with you."

"Amen. I couldn't have said it better. You don't know what's going to happen, Yaz, but you have to give it a chance. I mean, if you're feeling him, and I know you are, then stop being stupid and own that title. If he messes up, leave, but don't penalize him and he hasn't done anything. That's just stupid, and it's not fair."

"The fuck you in here complaining about now?" Miego asked when he entered the room. He walked past all of them and leaned over Ray to see what she was doing.

"Mind your business. We're not complaining, we're having a discussion about how men do dumb stuff," Yami said with a smirk

"Why you looking at me like that? You said do dumb stuff, and that ain't me, shorty. So I know you ain't talking 'bout me. Shit, you must be talking 'bout them." Miego pointed at Train and Memphis who had entered right behind him.

"They're not talking 'bout me either, shit." Train walked over to Lisa and lifted his son from her arms before sitting down next to her on the sofa. He held Tavion in the air and starting grinning at him.

"Don't say anything when he throws up in your face," Lisa said and rolled her eyes before she leaned forward to place his empty bottle on the table in front of her.

"You not gon' throw up on daddy, are you, lil man?" Tavion grinned, which made Train smile even harder.

"You need to be talking about why the hell she can't grow up and act like a damn adult," Memphis said, glaring at Yaz.

"Really, Memphis? You're the one pouting like a little kid because you can't have your way. But that's cool, though."

Miego kissed Ray on the cheek and then walked back over to them. "I told you not to fuck with her. She be on some shit, bruh. What you do, Yaz?"

"Mind your business," Yaz said, rolling her eyes at Miego.

"Shit, we family, and you're fucking with my boy, so your business is my business," Miego said with a grin before he pulled Yami to her feet, took her seat and then forced her into his lap.

"You know what? All of you can kiss my ass. I'm not in the mood, and this isn't even about you." Yaz jumped up and left the room.

Memphis waved her off. Yami got up to follow her sister, but Miego stopped her. "Chill, I got it. I'm the one that pissed her off. Let me go holla at sis for a minute."

Yami scrunched her face up like she was undecided about allowing him to go talk to Yaz, which he sensed before he playfully mushed her. "I got this, man. You act like I can't be civil and shit, damn."

"Somebody needs to talk to her indecisive ass, cause she's not trying to hear me."

"I got you, bruh." He kissed Yami, and was on his way to find Yaz.

The second she laid her eyes on him, she rolled them. "What, Miego? I'm not in the mood for your rude ass," Yaz said as she yanked open the refrigerator and looked inside.

"Yo, calm all that down. I'm not Memphis, Yaz. I just came to see what's up. You good?"

"Absolutely fucking perfect," she said after she had a beer in her hand and was facing him. She twisted the cap off and leaned against the counter.

"What's up, Yaz, why you tripping?"

She looked at him and released a sarcastic laugh. "Don't act like you care."

"Man, gone with that. If I didn't care, I wouldn't be asking your dumb ass. So what's up?"

Yaz looked at him and laughed again. He was always so damn rude, even when he was trying to be nice, which clearly, he was trying to do in his own way. She didn't know why, but she decided to roll with it.

"He just wants too much too fast. I don't see the point."

She waited and watched Miego. She could tell that he was thinking, which wasn't like him. Usually, what came up came out, so she was curious as to what he was about to say.

"What's too much too fast?"

"Like, with us, I don't get why we can't just chill for a minute. Everything has to be so serious."

Miego chuckled. "Y'all females be on some shit, yo. You got my man trying to lock shit down, and you act like he doing something crazy. Then, when you can't get his ass to commit, you're running around crying about he ain't no damn good. Make up your mind. For real. We can't do shit right cause y'all be confused as fuck. How the hell we supposed to rock with that bipolar shit?" He looked right at her like he really expected her to respond to that.

"I knew better than to even go there with you," Yaz said, pulling her body from the counter.

Just before she was about to move past him, he caught her arm. "Calm your little ass down. I'm saying some real shit. Just listen. Memphis is a good dude. He ain't one of them pussy ass muthafuckers that I know you and your sister like to fuck with. The same way she got something real with me, you got something real with my dude. I know him, Yaz, if he's pushing you to make shit legit then he's ready. He's not on any bullshit, so rock with him. He won't fuck you over unless you give him a reason to."

"That's your boy, so you could tell me anything."

"I could, but I wouldn't. You know me by now, and you know I say what the fuck I mean. You might not always like what I say, but I ain't never lied to you, and I'm not about to start now. He's a good dude,

Yaz, and you aight. You get on my damn nerves most of the time, but you're fam, so I wouldn't steer you wrong. I put that on everything."

Yaz stared at him for a minute and then burst out laughing.

"The fuck you laughing for?"

"Cause this ain't you." She waved her hand at him with a huge smile plastered all over her face. For the first time, she could see a glimpse of why her sister was so gone over him. Underneath his harsh exterior, he was actually a good guy. Yaz knew that, but seeing it up close and personal made it more real.

"Man, fuck outta here with that. I can be nice when I want to, I just don't like your ass, so I'm not. Now quit acting like a damn baby and go fix shit with my boy."

Yaz shook her head and laughed before placing her beer on the counter. She stepped to Miego and peered at him before he pulled her into a hug, let her go, and then mushed her in the head.

"Yo, spoiled ass. Just like your damn sister. I swear y'all worse than Ray."

He winked at Yaz and then left her in the kitchen. She shook her head again, took a deep breath, and got ready to go deal with Memphis.

Chapter Six

"What?" Miego asked as he lifted Ray out of her car seat and waited for Yami to get Ray's backpack off the floor.

When they had everything they needed, he shut and locked the car doors and waited for Yami to stepped to his side. With Ray in one arm, he took Yami's hand with the other and the three of them headed into the building.

"Nothing," she said, smiling at him.

The fact that he had actually took time to help her sister figure things out with Memphis had her smiling inside. He tried to be so hard sometimes, but then this side of him came creeping out. Miego was constantly doing something that had her falling for him a little bit more every day, and the best part was that he wasn't even trying, or over the top with it. He just was who he was.

"Then why you keep looking at me like that, shorty? That shit is creepy as fuck, yo."

When they reached their door, Yami used her keys to open it. Miego waited and let her enter first while he was right behind her.

"So me looking at you is creepy?" Yami asked after she placed Ray's backpack on the counter and then followed him down the hall to her daughter's room.

He laid Ray on the bed, kissed her cheek, and then stepped away while Yami began to remove her shoes.

"It is when you just looking at me but not saying shit," he said, which made her laugh. "I'm about to head in this studio for a minute."

"I'll be in there after I get her changed." Yami grinned at him while leaving Ray's bed to get her something to sleep in.

Miego left, and she got her daughter changed before going to find him. When she entered his studio, she watched him leaning over his sound board, nodding to whatever he was listening to. She sat down across from him and pulled her feet up then tucked them under her butt, so that she was comfortable in the chair.

He looked up at her and winked, but kept working. She watched him as he punched, pulled, and moved switches. He always got into a zone, and watching him move was sexy to her. Like now, he was biting down into his lip, with an intense look on his face, like he was deep in thought. It only lasted for a minute until he made a few adjustments and then a smile spread across his face.

She loved everything about him, and it was evident that she simply loved him. Even if neither of them had said it out loud, she knew it was true.

Instead of bothering him, she sat there watching for a while before she decided to go hop in the shower. The second he saw her move, one of his hands was on her waist, while the other pulled his headphones off.

"Where you going?"

"To shower."

"Hold up, I'm coming," he said.

"No, finish what you're doing." Yami placed her hands on the side of his face, stroking his beard with her thumbs before she let her lips connect with his.

"I won't be long. I just want to finish this really quick." He nodded toward his soundboard, but kept his eyes on her as if waiting for approval to stay. He knew how easy it was for him to get lost in his music, and he never wanted her to feel put off.

"I'll come get you if you get lost." Yami pecked him on the lips once more before leaving and shutting the door behind her.

She made her way to their bedroom to shower and get ready for bed, grinning the whole time because thoughts of Miego filled her head. It had been a long day; school, and then dinner at Train's house. Now that she was home, all she wanted to do was relax.

After her shower, she dressed and climbed in bed, armed with the remote and hugging a pillow. What she thought was going to be TV time turned into lights out because the second her head hit the pillow, she drifted and didn't wake up again until she felt Miego pulling her body against his.

"That's how we doing it? You just gon' crash on me, shorty?"

Yami opened her eyes when she felt his lips on the side of her face, and his hands roaming her body. She was dressed in only a t-shirt and panties. He had full access, and was taking advantage of it.

"I was tired," she mumbled, snuggling closer to him.

Letting her hands move across his arm, up his shoulder, and then to his neck, she slid one of her legs between his, and felt his erection the second she had it in place.

"Nah, not yet, but you're about to be."

Miego's hand moved to the back of her head, tangling it in her hair before his lips connected with hers. Sending his tongue into her mouth, their kiss got deeper and more intense until he broke away and forced her on her back. His body moved over hers while his hands moved up her stomach, taking her shirt with them until her body was exposed. He began a trail of kisses from her chest to her waist. Once he reached her center, he planted a series of kisses through the thin material covering it, and then moved his thumb in the waistband, pulling them down her thighs until she was able to slide her legs out of them.

Using his large hands to spread her legs apart, he just stared at her hidden treasure for a minute, grinning while she watched him. She was damn near holding her breath with the anticipation building because he never showed mercy when he had his head between her legs.

"Why you look scared, shorty? You nervous? You should be used to this by now."

Yami laughed. "Why would I be scared?"

Miego chuckled and lowered his head, getting as close as he could without touching her. "Because we both know you can't hang."

His voice vibrated against her thighs and his breath on her sweetness caused an instant reaction, which was his signal to do damage. His fingers glided across her exposed skin, just enough to cause her body to shiver before he moved two inside her and his tongue caressed her clit. Eager to please, he began to gently suck on it, which had Yami fighting against him.

The way she squirmed, trying to push him away, was more motivation to go harder, so he used his free hand to grip her thigh to hold her in place. She eventually gave up and allowed him full control over her body. It didn't take long for the explosion to take place, and she lay helpless, in recovery from the massive orgasm that had plummeted through her body.

He took the opportunity to remove his boxers and then climbed between her legs, but she stopped him by sitting up and forcing him over onto his back. His eyes were on her as she scaled his body, starting at his chest and then moving down below his waist. When her lips met the head of his throbbing erection, a moan escaped his lips.

"Fuck, Yami, you trying to end this shit early, shorty."

Miego's eyes were closed and his hand moved though her hair. With a fist full of it and a little pressure, he began guiding her movements. It wasn't that she needed the help, he just couldn't control it because she was killing him with the slow sensual way she moved up and down his shaft. She was always so detailed and concise that he could barely stand it, which she did on purpose because it was the only time she had control over him.

Thrusting his hips aggressively toward her, he sped up the motion, and it only took minuets for his nut to reach the surface. Wanting to release his first one inside of her, Miego yanked her head back and pulled her toward him, guiding her down onto his erection. With a satisfied grin on her face, she began rotating her hips, and seconds later, he gripped her waist and released inside her.

"Fuck, shorty, keep moving," Miego instructed and she did.

Once he was at his full potential again, his hands were on her waist, but he flipped her over.

"Sit up, Yamiah," he demanded as he moved behind her, pulling her body against his. The second she was on her knees, he plunged in from behind without notice.

"Miego, wait." Her hands covered her stomach as she felt the pressure from him being so deep inside her.

"Nah, shorty. You good."

Miego slid his arm loosely around her neck, holding her against his chest, and plunged in an out of her body so aggressively that she could barely breathe. She gripped his arm to brace herself, but enjoyed every inch he offered. There were days when Miego was slow and steady, and days when he just wanted to fuck, and right now, he wanted to fuck.

After multiple orgasms and her body on the verge of shutting down, she heard Miego grunt really loud into her neck. He held her so tight that she felt like he was squeezing every last bit of energy out of her that she had left before he let her go and collapsed onto his side, breathing out of control.

"You gon' fuck around and kill my ass." Miego pulled her down toward him and held her close to his body, kissing her neck and shoulder in the process.

"That was all you, not me." Yami smiled as she moved her hand across his abs.

"Nah, that was that bomb ass pussy. It dictates everything I do, shorty. Fuck what you heard." Miego chuckled at his own words.

"You just remember that when you have all those women in your face offering you other options."

"Man, chill with that shit." Miego lifted his hand and mushed her in the head. "Can't nobody fuck with what you offering. Trust me, Yamiah. I'm not even 'bout to set myself up to get disappointed."

"Whatever, you say that now."

"I say that now, then, and forever, so stop with all that and take your ass to sleep. I would go shower, but I don't wanna have to carry your little ass, so we'll get that shit in the morning. I know your damn legs weak as fuck right now."

Miego smirked and sat up enough to grab the covers and throw them across their naked bodies.

"Asshole."

Yami slapped his chest and then snuggled closer to him. He was partially right. She could move if she absolutely had to, but it would be difficult. So for now, she accepted his offer to just go to sleep, and that was exactly what the two of them did. Within minutes, they were tangled against each other's bodies and out like a light.

Chapter Seven

Yami had been up since seven, trying to make sure that she had everything ready for Ray's party. Her baby girl was turning three, and as excited as she was about that, coordinating everything for her party was driving her insane. Ray was dead set on a princess theme, and it was exhausting trying to get everything she needed to make it happen.

On top of that, she had to try and make sure everyone could be there, and that in itself was a headache. Between Miego's family and hers, it was almost impossible to find the time to make it happen, so she finally just picked a date and told everyone else to make it work.

She wanted everyone there, but it was about Ray being happy, and that was far more important than trying to adjust things to fit everyone else's schedules. The problem was that the only guests would be family and two other kids from her daycare.

Yami sat on the floor looking at the sea of pink and purple stuff that surrounded her. She was in the process of putting together gift baskets for Ray and her two friends. What should have been an easy task had gotten really complicated because she'd over done it with the stuff that she purchased for it. Princess Barbie dolls, tiaras, dress up clothes, shoes and jewelry, and more candy than a child should eat in a year.

She was really tempted to just dump it all in the sequined covered baskets that she purchased and hand it to them, but she was a fanatic about presentation. So here she was, trying to figure out a way to get everything in the baskets she purchased and make it look presentable.

"Mommy, can I help?" Ray asked, running in the room with Miego right behind her.

"No, Ray, let me do it, but you can get all of this crap out of here so that they can set up the tables."

"But I'm playing with it," Ray whined, looking down at the dolls and accessories that were all over the living room floor.

"Ray, no you're not. Just take them in your room, please. I don't have time to argue with you," Yami snapped, causing Ray to pout.

"Baby girl, go watch TV in your room for a little while and let your mom finish this. I'll get this stuff for you."

Ray looked at her mother and then at Miego before she turned on her heels and left them in the living room, but she was pouting the entire time.

"Why you tripping? Don't get mad at Ray 'cause you over did it with all this shit. I told you to let me pay somebody to do it."

Yami rolled her eyes at him and leaned back, covering her face with her hands. "I'm not mad because I want her to clean up her mess."

Miego chuckled before kneeling down enough to move her arms from her face and kiss her lips.

"Call your sister and Yanna to come help you with this shit. I told you it was too much, but don't be snapping at baby girl 'cause you're hard headed."

"Shut up, I'm not hard headed. I just want it done right, so I'm doing it myself."

"Man, please, you stressed the fuck out and you are hardheaded. I could have easily paid somebody to put that shit together for you, but instead you're sitting here about to cry 'cause you're frustrated. Now go call your sister or I will."

Yami sucked her teeth and looked up at him. "That, I'm not worried about."

Miego started collecting all of Ray's toys and then took them to her room while Yami gave up and called in back up. She was over it, and ready to get everyone together, so if it was going to take Yaz and Yanna to do that, then that was what she was going to do. She still had to decorate, go pick up the cake, wait for the tables and food to arrive, on top of getting ready and getting Ray ready. She was over it, and willing to admit she had tried to do too much.

****

Hours later, everything was complete. Their apartment was full of people, and Ray was having the time of her life. She was the center of everyone's attention, just the way she liked it. As if she needed any more junk, all of their family and friends had over did it with presents for her, so that of course made it that much better. Simone had damn near purchased Ray an entire new summer wardrobe since the weather was getting warmer, along with matching outfits for the overpriced look alike doll she had custom made for Ray.

Train basically had gone through Toy R Us and purchased anything that looked remotely close to a princess theme, and Yanna had made sure to get Ray a kid sized mani and pedi station with every color or polish imaginable. Needless to say, Ray had way more than she needed, and that wasn't even including the things that Yami, Miego, and everyone else had purchased for her.

"Where the hell are we supposed to put all that shit?" Miego asked, pointing to the two tables full of Ray's presents. The tables were over flowing and the floor beneath them was lined with presents also.

Yami shrugged. "Her play room, I guess."

Since she and Miego were now in the master bedroom, her old room had been redecorated and changed into Ray's play room. It was already over flowing with junk even before today.

"Yeah, aight, I'd like to see you make that work."

"It's your fault. You bought most of this stuff," Yami said with a frown, which made him laugh because it was true.

"You right, but it's still on you to figure out how to make it fit."

"Not me, us. This is a team," Yami said.

"We're a team, but my focus is on making other stuff fit. I got that shit handled, so I'll let you have this."

Miego chuckled and walked off to go talk to Train and Memphis, who were grouped up in the living room. This gave Sylvia a chance to harass her daughter. She had been waiting since she got there for the chance to give her opinion about Yami and Miego's lifestyle. Yami had been avoiding her all day, not wanting to ruin her mood or Ray's party, but she knew it was coming.

"Well, I guess you're living the fairytale life, huh? Is that what you're teaching Rayah? Because this isn't real life, Yamiah."

"Ma, don't start."

"Start what, Yamiah? I'm not starting anything, just asking a question. I'm entitled to my opinion, right?"

Yami looked up and caught her sister's eye, and Yaz started toward the two of them.

"You're entitled to your opinion, but why does it always have to be so negative? I'm happy, Ray's happy, just leave it alone. It's not about fairytales."

"That's what it looks like, perfect man, perfect life, plenty of money. I hope you don't think this will last forever, because it won't."

"Why are you so hateful? It's like you want us to be miserable. I love you, Ma, but you need to get a life. Maybe if you had one then you wouldn't have to spend so much time hatin' on ours. It's your granddaughter's birthday and you're over here worrying about something that isn't any of your business," Yaz said, coming to her sister's defense.

"How is it not my business when my daughter is caught up with a man like that? The second everything falls apart, she's going to be right back in my house staring in my face, begging for me to take care of her. And the same goes for you. I see you're following right behind her, Yazmine."

"You know what? If I lost all this tomorrow, I promise you one thing, I would never come to you for help. I'd figure it out on my own because I see now that you're more concerned with seeing me failing than succeeding. I'm over that. You don't like the way I live, then leave. You don't have to be here. There's a room full of people who support me and Ray, so if you feel like that's too much for you to do, then you don't have to be here."

Yami was in her mother's face with her finger inches away from her forehead. She was almost yelling because she was so annoyed, which got Miego's attention, along with everyone else's in the room.

He had a scowl on his face as he made his way over to her. "What's going on?"

Sylvia looked up at him with disgust before she laughed. "You here to rescue her again? How many more you got in you before you figure out that she' not worth rescuing?"

Yami's mouth flew open as her eyes moved around the room. Everyone had eyes on them, even though they were pretending not to be interested in the conversation, simply for the fact that they felt her pain. She noticed Ginette's face, and when their eyes met, she offered a sympathetic smile as she held Ray in her arms.

"No disrespect, but this is my house and you're not gonna talk to her like that in here. And for the record, it's foul as shit that you can't just be happy for your own daughter. Who the fuck does that? But don't worry, she's good. I got her and so do they." He pointed to his family. "It's fucked up that my mother is more of a mother to your daughter than you are, so if you wanna judge, take your ass over there to that mirror and start there first."

"Miego, don't be disrespectful," Ginette said, moving closer to her son. She knew that he was right, but it was still Yami's mother, and she didn't want her son to be rude.

"Nah, fuck her, Ma. I apologize to you because I know you not feeling the way I said it, but I meant every word. She's foul as fuck, and that shit ain't necessary."

Sylvia's mouth dropped open and she looked at both of her daughters, expecting them to defend her, but neither of them spoke up. In fact, Yaz folded her arms and looked at her like she was waiting for a reply.

"Fine, I guess you got your own little happy family, so there's no need for me to be here." She stared at Yami and Yaz for a second before she started to walk off.

"That's your choice, not hers. She needs you, but not like this, and I'm not gon' sit here and watch somebody I love constantly get broken down because you can't get your feelings in check. That shit ain't happening," Miego said.

"That's how you feel?" Sylvia turned and was now focused on Yami.

"Ma, I love you, I swear I do, but he's right. I need you, but not if it means that you can't figure out a way to be okay with the choices I make for me and Ray."

"Yeah, well like I said, this won't last forever. Just remember that." Sylvia, looked at Ginette with a snide smile. "Congratulations, you have a daughter," was the last thing she said before storming to the door, grabbing her purse off the table next to it, and leaving.

Everyone watched, but didn't say a word.

Yaz hugged her sister and then kissed her on the cheek. "She'll figure it out, or she won't. Either way, we're good. You have me."

Yami laughed to mask the hurt she was feeling. "Oh lord, I'm in trouble then."

"See, every time I try to be nice to you, you act like an ass."

Yaz shoved her sister and then hugged her again. When she let her go, Miego grabbed her hand and took her down the hall to their bedroom. He just wanted a minute alone with her because he was pissed about the show her mother had just put on, but he knew she was hurt, and he wanted to make sure she was good without everyone's eyes on them.

"I'm fine." Yami said as soon as he shut the door.

"That was some fucked up shit, so if you're not, it's cool. I just wanted to check on you.

Yami shrugged. "I can't change it, so..."

"You're right, and you don't have to deal with it either."

"I just don't get it. I guess that's why it bothers me so much."

"I feel you, shorty, but like I said. It's not for you to get. Some people just can't see past their own shit long enough to consider someone else. Honestly, she loves you. She's your mother so she has to, but she got her own shit to deal with. What that is, I don't know, and I really don't give a fuck, but it's preventing her from being happy with you. I know you keep trying, and I respect you for that, but when the shit affects your happiness, I can't rock with it."

Yami smiled as she searched his face. He was by the door a few feet away from her and he looked like he was ready to hurt someone. It made her think about what he said to her mother about not letting her hurt someone he loved.

She bit her bottom lip and then looked right into his eyes. They were so intense because he was angry, but like always, they softened as she stared at him.

"I know, and I'm done for now. I just which she would figure it out." Yami moved to him and let her arms slide around his waist before he leaned down to kiss her.

"This is life, Yamiah. It damn sure ain't no fairytale, but I promise you this much, ain't shit I won't do for you or Ray. As long as I'm physically able, I'll be here for you. That's my word, and you can bet your life on that."

Yami smiled because she believed him. He didn't have to convince her of that anymore because he had already done it a million times over. So she just lifted her weight onto the balls of her feet and kissed him again. "I love you too."

A smile spread across his face and he looked down at her. "I didn't say shit about loving you, shorty."

Yami laughed. "Yes, you did, you just don't realize you said it."

"When?"

"Let's go. I know everybody's looking for us." She stepped around him and was about to open the door, but he caught her arm and pulled her back into his body.

After another kiss, his lips grazed the side of her face before he spoke again. "Don't make me regret giving you my heart, shorty."

Yami smiled and looked up at him. "I told you, if you got me, I got you."

They rejoined their guests and enjoyed the rest of Ray's party without any other incidents. Ginette made sure to pull Yami to the side to let her know her feelings about the situation and to reassure her that she always had someone. In no way was she attempting to replace her mother, but she promised to be there for her in any way Yami needed her to be.

The rest of the day went smoothly without incident, and Ray was pleased. That was all that mattered. Even with her mother's insanity, the day was still a good day and that was worth all the heartache that went into making it happen.

Chapter Eight

"What's up, shorty?" Miego smiled when he heard Yami's voice flow through his car.

He was sitting outside of Ray's daycare about to pick her up and spend the rest of the day with her. Yami didn't know it yet, but at his mother's request, he had set up time for Yami, Yanna, and his mom to chill. Yanna had insisted on a spa day, so he paid for the three of them to have some girl time.

"I'm just leaving campus. I think I totally bombed my test."

He could hear the pouty undertone in her voice and laughed. "Man, you say that every time, Yamiah, and then you ace that shit. Why you always stressing? You were up all night with them damn books everywhere, so I'm sure you did fine, with your Urkel ass."

"That's not funny. I really don't think so this time."

"Yeah, aight. You wanna put money on it?"

Yami laughed. "Why is everything always a bet with you?"

"Because I'm always right, so I might as well get money for my knowledge. But check it, head to my mom's spot. I'm about to get Ray. I'm taking her to Wild Zone so she can empty my pockets for a minute."

"Wait, why? I'll just come meet you guys there."

"No hell you won't. Ginette is expecting you, and I'm not trying to have her in my shit because you didn't show up."

"But you didn't even ask me." She was okay with spending time with Ginette, but today she had her mind set on getting Ray and heading home to chill with Miego. It was the norm, and what she was used to.

"The fuck I need to ask you for? When my moms request your time, you just roll with it, shorty. Chill, and go have fun," Miego said with a huge smile because he knew she was stressing about it.

"Fun, what do you mean have fun?" Yami questioned. If she was just going to his mother's house, then what was fun about that? They would just catch up and talk like they usually did. It wasn't a bad thing, but fun wasn't a word you would use.

"Man, just take your whiny ass to my mom's house. They're waiting on you."

"I hate you, you know that, right."

"Don't say no dumb shit like that, not even if you're playing, shorty." Yami could hear the intensity in his voice, which made her smile.

"I really don't like you right now? Is that better?"

"Man, gone before you make me cuss you out. Have fun, and I love your punk ass too."

Yami laughed because he had yet to really tell her that he loved her, even though she knew he did. He made it clear by dancing around the subject, but he'd never really just come out and said it. She was good with that though because the words didn't mean as much as the actions, in her opinion, but she had to mess with him.

"You love me, Miego?"

"Why the hell you ask me some shit you already know the answer to?"

"Say it then." Yami couldn't hold the giggles that were escaping.

"Didn't I just say that shit, man? I'm not fucking with you, Yamiah. Let me go so that I can get my baby girl. We got a date and you fucking around," Miego said playfully. He hadn't really gotten used to saying it, but she knew, so he wasn't stressing over it.

They ended the call and Yami changed courses and headed to meet Ginette and Yanna. She didn't know what they had planned, so she was prepared for anything. When she got there, she parked and made her way to his mother's apartment. The second Yanna pulled the door open, she and his mother were on their feet with their purses in hand, since Miego had sent a text letting them know that Yami was on her way.

"Hey, boo. We have to go so we can make our appointment," Yanna said, rushing past Yami out the door. Ginette followed, but pulled Yami into a hug and kissed her cheek.

"Hello, sweetheart. I'm glad you're spending the day with us. I hope you don't mind."

"No, not at all. I just wished he had told me," Yami said as she waited for Yanna to lock their apartment door.

The three of them headed down the stairs, sticking close together. There was a junkie in the hallway who grabbed at Yanna's leg, but she kicked him and kept moving.

"I swear I hate it here, Ma. We really need to move. I don't know why you don't want to move," Yanna fussed as they pushed through the doors of their building to head outside.

"It's fine here. It's just somewhere to lay your head. Besides, the second you start doing too much, people will be asking questions and coming for your brother. There's no point in doing more than we need to."

"Ma, really. It's not that serious. It's not like we need a big house or something over the top, but it won't hurt to get out of here. We could move into the building where they live," Yanna said after she unlocked her car door to let them in.

"You could do that. It's nice, nothing over the top, but it's still nice." Yami shrugged and climbed in the back, letting Ginette, sit up front with her daughter.

"That fancy building you live in. Child, that place cost more than I've made my entire life. How could I explain that?"

"Ma, really. They don't know about every penny you made or saved. You worry too much, but we need to get out of that shitty ass building. It's not safe and I hate it. Miego keeps telling you that, and the only reason why he let it go is because you get so mad about it."

"They have smaller units than the one we have. It's really not that expensive. I think you should at least consider it. She's right, you know. It's not safe."

"Child, I ain't worried about those fools around there. They know better than to mess with me. I've been there so long, that there's no point in leaving now. I was the first person in that apartment. No one has ever lived there except me. That's my place."

Yami smiled at her persistence and hesitation about doing anything new. She understood her reasoning, but she wouldn't mind having them closer. She and Yanna were close now, and his mother was more of a mother to her than her own, not to mention the fact that Ray loved them both.

Their current place wasn't the best on the outside, but inside it was really nice. Miego made sure the furniture was new, well with the exception of her favorite floral chair that she refused to get rid of, and Ginette kept their place spotless. But it was time for them to move. The neighborhood was terrible, and not safe at all. Miego hated it, but didn't push because every time he did, it caused a huge argument about his lifestyle.

"Ma, you're so dang stubborn, I swear. But it's about to be my call and not yours. I'm over it. You can either come with me or stay where you are, but I'm moving," Yanna said with a frown on her face.

"Mmhmm, you ain't going nowhere," Ginette said in a way that caused Yami to laugh.

She knew that Ginette would have the final word, but Yanna wasn't going to make it easy.

****

"This place is nice, I know your brother didn't pick this," Yami said, looking around their private room. There were six stations set up and they occupied three of them. The ladies currently had their feet soaking in a foot bath while they were dressed in thick, pale blue robes. They had just finished their massages and were in the process of getting their mani-pedis.

"Girl, no, he just gave me money and said pay for it." Yanna laughed at the thought of her brother having to pick a spa for them to have a girls' day. It definitely wasn't his thing. He had a heart of gold, but some things just weren't going to change about him.

"You leave my baby alone. He could have, if he wanted to."

Yami smiled at Ginette defending her son. She loved her children like no other, and it made her a little jealous that she couldn't get that from her own mother.

"What's wrong, baby?"

"Nothing, just thinking."

"About? You know you can talk to me. That's what I'm here for. You're just as much my child as this one right here." She pointed to Yanna.

"I know, I guess that's the problem. I get more from you than I do my own mother." Yami was feeling a sense of sadness for the lack of relationship that she had with her mother.

"Sweetheart, as a mother, I can tell you this much. She loves you. I'm sure there's something going on with her internally that is affecting her ability to show it the way she needs to. But from what I can tell, her issues are getting in the way of her being what she needs to be for you. It's really hard to see past what you think and feel sometimes, especially when you are strong feelings about it. Trust me, I'm guilty of that myself.

"I don't love the lifestyle that my son has chosen, but it's his life. I just worry about him, about all of you, but I have to get past that because he's not going to change who he is, just because of how I feel about it. I push sometimes, but only because I love him and want him safe. I have to remember that it's his life and I can't live it for him. Your mother will realize that one day or maybe she won't, but until then, you have me. I know it's not the same, but I'm always here." She offered a comforting smile that for some reason made Yami feel better.

"And you have me too, boo. You're about to have a lot more of me as soon as we move into your building, so don't be hiding behind the door rolling your eyes when you check the security monitor and see it's me. You know I'm going to be bugging the hell out of you, so get ready," Yanna said with a cheesy grin, causing Yami to burst out laughing.

"Girl, you know I wouldn't do that. In fact, I'm kinda excited about it. I can go hide when your brother gets on my nerves."

"Mmhmm, hide my ass. You and I both know better than that. He ain't letting you out of his sight for long. You or Ray, and you know it, but that sounded good. I swear, you had a lot of confidence when it came out your mouth. If I didn't know my brother, I might have actually believed you." Yanna laughed, but more to herself, thinking about how possessive her brother had become over Ray and Yami. It was cute to her, and something she never saw happening. She was just glad that he was happy.

"Well, I don't think any of that will be a problem because we're not moving," Ginette said, shaking her head with a partial frown.

"Whatever, ma. Just watch." Yanna let her head fall back and closed her eyes. Yami did the same.

The spa day turned out perfect, and just what all of them needed. When they arrived back at their building, Ginette went upstairs and Yanna stopped Yami before she was about to leave. She had a few things on her mind and wanted to run them by her.

"Can I ask you a personal question?" Yanna looked so serious that Yami wasn't really sure if she would be ready for it.

"Sure, what's up?"

"So, you know about me and Renz, right?"

Yami smiled assuming this was about to be a question about relationship advice. She definitely wasn't the one to give it, considering how her past choices hadn't been that great. But she was just happy that Yanna trusted her enough to ask.

"Yeah, are you guys good?"

Yanna's smile told the story before the words even left her mouth. "Yes, that's the problem. We're at that place." Her smile faded a little and she looked stressed.

"Oh gosh, Yanna. I'm not having this conversation with you. Anything remotely related to you and a boy will cause your brother to kill us both." Yami laughed really hard at the thought of her giving Yanna advice about sex.

"Ain't nobody worried 'bout him. Don't tell him. This is between me and you, and I don't know what to do."

Yami raised her eyebrows and her expression when flat. "Wait, are you a virgin?"

"Dang, don't say it like it's a disease or something." Yanna's face balled up as she looked out into their neighborhood.

Yami laughed at how intense Yanna got. The two of them were only months different in age, and here Yami was with a three-year-old daughter and Yanna was a virgin. It wasn't a big deal, but it made her process how different the two of them were.

"I'm sorry. I just didn't really think about it, but I guess knowing who your brother is, I can see why." Yami teased.

"Exactly. He's a walking slut bucket, no disrespect, but wants to shoot any man that even smiles at me."

"Girl, none taken. I have no say over what his life was like before me, and we're good as long as he knows that shit won't fly now."

"He knows, trust me. I've never seen my brother the way he is with you. It's weird as hell, like really weird."

"Good, and he better stay that way," Yami said firmly.

"Trust me, you have nothing to worry about, but I do, so tell me what to do. It's like we get there, and then I just don't know if I'm ready to cross that line yet. I mean, I want to, I really do, but then again I don't know."

"What's he say about it?"

"He says he's good with waiting, but I can tell he's frustrated. What I don't want is for him to get it somewhere else because he can't get it from me."

"Don't let that be the reason. That's how I ended up with Ray. I was young and stupid, and thought that sex would be enough to make a cheater faithful. I knew who Black was when I started messing with him, and I still went into it thinking that there was something about me that could change him. I love Ray, but if I could do it all over again, I would have never crossed that line with him. Not because of her, but because he didn't deserve me. So don't do it because you think you'll lose him if you don't."

Yanna was quiet for a minute. "You're right, but it's not just that. I want to. I mean, he's sexy as hell, and when we're close like that, I swear every inch of my body is going off the charts. So it's not like I don't want to, I guess I just don't want it to change things."

"Oh, boo, it's gonna change things. Good or bad, things will definitely be different, so be prepared for that. Once you cross that line, there's no going back, though."

"So, one more question." Yanna wore a smirk.

"I think he might be a little more than I can handle."

Yami looked at Yanna for a minute, a little thrown by her statement, and then laughed. "Wait, why do you say that?"

"Because it's not like he tries to hide it. Hell, he couldn't if he wanted to."

"You'll be fine. It might take some adjusting. If you do decide to take it there, don't give up after your first time. Contrary to what everyone says, that shit will have you rethinking all of your life choices if it's anything like mine. I promise you, I was convinced that it would be my first and last."

Yanna frowned. "I hope you don't think that was supposed to help."

"Girl, trust me. It takes time to figure things out and learn your body. Just give it time, and don't get pregnant. Oh lord, don't get pregnant. Your brother would die."

Yanna laughed. "Umm, no I would die because he would kill me and Renz both. Trust me, if I make that decision, I will definitely be smart about it. I'm not trying to die just yet."

The two talked for a little while longer before they said their goodbyes and Yami was on her way home. She was all smiles at the fact that Yanna had come to her for advice. She wasn't sure how much she helped, and lord knows Miego would have killed her if he knew the advice she gave. At this point, it was about what Yanna needed, and not what he wanted. It was her life, and hopefully he wouldn't find out and kill them both.

Chapter Nine

"Man, you need to stop your damn lying. You know you're not going. You talking big shit, and the second sis starts with that pouting, you'll be like, 'bruh, I'll catch y'all next time.'" Train waved Miego off which made him and Memphis both laugh.

"Fuck you, Train. I said I'm going and I'm going. The fuck you think this is?"

"What I think is your ass is whipped like no other, and you can't be out past midnight."

"Damn, Miego, it's like that?"

"Hell no."

He laughed before he continued because it was close to the truth. It wasn't that he couldn't be out, he just didn't want to. He was perfectly content being home with Yami and Ray every night. The streets didn't offer anything but trouble, and he wasn't about to let anything or anyone fuck up his happy home.

"I'm a grown ass man and I run my house, so if I wanna be out, I can. I just choose not to. Just cause your hoe ass be tricking every night don't mean that I need to be."

Train turned up the glass he was holding, and after finishing off the contents, he laughed. "Fuck you mean. That shit sounded gay as hell. I be fucking bitches, not tricking. Got me sounding like I'm on a corner or some shit like that."

"What the fuck ever. Point being, your ass ain't doing nothing I wanna be connected to. I keep telling you, you better stop fucking around on Lisa. She gon' mess around and leave your hoe ass on some real shit. Just cause y'all share a kid don't mean she gon' keep putting up with your bullshit, yo."

"This mutherfucker here," Memphis said with a grin.

"What muthafucker? I see you calmed your shit down too. You ain't fucking with nobody but Yaz annoying ass, so don't you say shit."

Memphis just laughed because it was true. For the first time in a long time, he was only rocking with one person. He had never been what you would call a cheater, it was just that he hadn't really been in what was classified as a relationship until he started dealing with Yaz.

"That's what the fuck I thought," Miego said aggressively after Memphis just smiled but didn't try to defend his situation with Yaz.

"Lisa ain't going nowhere. She's a lot of things, but crazy ain't one of them," Train said confidently.

He knew they were right though and he needed to get his shit together. It just wasn't that simple. He was addicted to women, being with just one wasn't something he saw happening. He loved Lisa, and he loved their son even more, but it was hard as hell to imagine only being with her. He'd tried it several times and always ended up slipping.

"Yeah, keep thinking that. I promise you gon' regret it. Get your shit together."

Train shook his head before he sat up and grabbed the bottle of Hennessy that was on the table in front of him. The three were currently chilling at Memphis's house while they discussed plans for the evening. Yami, Yanna, Yaz and Lisa had a girls' night planned, which freed the three of them up for the night. There was a party happening that they were considering falling through. It had been a minute since Miego and Train had hit the streets like that, but they figured what the hell. It was time to unwind and chill. Business was good, which meant that money was flowing, and their personal lives were on point, so one night was much needed and deserved.

"It's a house party, right?" Memphis asked, looking for more detail. He wasn't from their neighborhood but he rocked with Train and Miego. Other than that, he didn't really know anybody else.

"Yeah, they throw that shit a few times a year. It's usually pretty chill, even with all the muthafuckers who don't fuck with each other. Everybody usually does their own thing, plenty of women, liquor, and every high you can think of, so muthafuckers be squashing beefs just for the night," Miego said, offering up details about the event.

"Hell yeah. Last time they did that shit, they brought in strippers from four states to do their thing. Shit was on point," Train added.

"There you go with that shit. You just don't learn," Miego said.

"Yo, you do you and I'll do me. What about Tron, though? What he been up to? If Yanna chillin' with the girls, see if he wanna hang." Train chuckled before turning up his glass.

"Oh fuck no. He don't need to be nowhere near that shit. He's inches away from getting the fuck outta here, and the last thing he needs is to be around that bullshit." Miego made a point of looking out for his brother, which meant keeping him away from certain things, and parties like this was damn sure one of them.

"Shit, you right. I ain't think about that. Besides, he's whipped just like your ass, so he probably wouldn't go anyway. Jai and Tajh got him on lockdown."

Miego chuckled, thinking about his brother's relationship. He never understood it until Yami was in his life. "You right, but that's good for him. He's right where he needs to be."

"So we doing that shit, then?" Memphis eyed both Train and Miego.

He was down for one night with them, and he planned to have fun, but he damn sure wasn't crossing any lines that he couldn't recover from. There wasn't anything wrong with seeing a few asses in action, though.

"I'm down. That's on him," Train said.

"Shit, it's whatever," Miego offered.

He was down for a night out, but like Memphis, he had no plans to fuck up his happy home.

"Aight then, I guess we making moves later then. But on another note, I been keeping an eye on Lena, and that bitch crazy. I mean, I get she sad and shit about her sister, but she doing too much. Her ass lives at the fucking precinct. I don't know what the fuck she be doing up there, but if that bitch ain't at the hospital, then she's up there. I even saw her hoe ass at lunch with that damn detective," Train said, causing Miego's pulse to race.

Miego had been civil and stayed away from it because he knew that if he got anywhere near her dumb ass, there was going be another funeral in her family. But hearing what Train was telling him had him rethinking his decision.

"The fuck you mean she's been at the precinct? She fucking dude or' what? Man, I need to pay her ass a visit. I don't have time for no more bullshit."

"Oh, fuck no, bruh. You stay the hell away from her or I'll shoot you my got damn self. Shit, we already got two bodies hanging in the wind, and we damn sure don't need three. Not to mention another one of them is a got damn cop. We already got away with that shit one time, so I ain't taking no more chances. Let that bitch do what the fuck she wants. It's been months, and if they haven't come for you already, then they're not. They don't have shit, right?" Memphis asked.

"Nah, they don't have shit, but seems like she still trying. Fuck outta here with that shit," Miego yelled.

"Yo, I'm telling you, stay the fuck away from her. The cop that put you under, and the witness that helped him put you there ended up dead. The only reason they didn't pin that shit on you is because they couldn't, but the fuck you think gon' happen if her sister ends up dead too? And if she fucking that cop, we gon' have to handle his ass also. You can be mad all you want, Miego, but on God you better keep your hostile ass away from her." Train didn't flinch or break his stare because he meant every word.

He knew Miego, and he knew how badly he wanted to handle Lena for putting Yami in the middle of things. Then to add fuel to the fire, Lena had even had nerve to run up on Yami. Lena ending up dead was a bad move, and one that Miego wouldn't be able to walk away from.

Miego looked at Train and Memphis, and they both looked seconds away from filling his ass full of lead if it meant keeping him away from Lena. He was mad as hell, but had to laugh at the seriousness behind both of their demands.

"Yo, why the fuck every time I got a problem, both of y'all bitch asses start telling me how the fuck I can handle it with all that we shit? I ain't ask neither one of you to do a got damn thing."

"This muthafucker here," Memphis said for the second time that day. "Look, you held me down when we were in the cage on some real shit. I was locked up with every muthafucker I had ever done dirty, and you had my back. We both walked out that bitch alive and well, so yeah, *we*."

"Man, I ain't even gon' say shit, 'cause you already know. But I promise you this, you take your ass anywhere near Lena, and this we is gon' be simplified to me and Memphis 'cause you won't be around anymore. Ray will be calling me uncle-daddy."

Miego and Memphis both burst out laughing, which made Train laugh. "Shit, I'm just saying. I gotta look out for baby girl since he insists on trying to do shit that might put his dumb ass back in that cage."

"Yo, fuck you and him." Miego pointed at Train first and then Memphis. "Ray is the only thing keeping that bitch alive. I fucked up one time with baby girl already, and I'm all she's got. I'm not gon' make her lose both her fathers."

No matter what feelings Miego had about Black, it still fucked him up that getting rid of him meant that Ray was losing something. That was a demon he was struggling with, but he had to make peace with it the best he could. The only way he knew how was to make sure Ray never wanted or needed for anything. Not just material things, but emotionally as well. He planned on being any and everything she needed without question.

"That's what the fuck I thought, but I'm 'bout to head out, though. Lisa hit me with that we need to talk bullshit this morning, and since she gon' be with both of y'all happy ass wives later, I need to get her head right."

"Nah, her head ain't the one you need to get right, but good luck with that shit," Miego said, pointing at Train.

The three chilled for a little while longer before they parted ways. Each one had to get their time in before they hit the streets later, so for now it was time to go play house.

****

When Miego walked in their apartment, he found Yami sitting on the sofa with her elbows propped up on her knees and her head lowered in her hand. She didn't bother looking up at him, so he knew that something was up. He made his way over and sat down in front of her, taking her hands away from her face.

"Yamiah, what's wrong?"

Her eyes were red and swollen and her nose and cheeks were tinted a shade of red from her rubbing them, due to her light complexion. She stared at him, not really knowing how to explain that her heart was breaking for her daughter, because of him. Ray had been asking about her father on and off lately, but right before he came home, she had a complete meltdown and it had Yami all messed up.

She had tried to explaining to Ray that her father was gone, but the questions kept rolling, and she was at a loss trying to explain to her three year old why she would never see her father again. That lasted until Ray took off to her room in tears, which Yami let her do alone because she didn't know how to fix it or make it right.

"Ray wants to know why she can't see her father," came out barely above a whisper, but her eyes were on his in a way that had him wanting to just grab her and hold her. He fought the urge and stayed put.

"Where is she?" His eyes left Yami's long enough to scan the room before they were on Yami again.

"In her room."

"What did you tell her?"

Yami's shoulders were slumped slightly, but she shrugged them a little. "Nothing, really. What can I tell her? She usually asks and I tell her he's not here anymore and then she lets it go, but this time she wanted to know where he was and when he was coming back. She kept telling me to take her to Simone's house because he always came to see her there."

"Fuck." Miego mumbled under his breath.

He knew it was coming, but so far they'd skated by without really having to explain things to her. She was so small that it was easy to get her side tracked or keep her occupied. And the fact that she had so many people in her life who were constantly with her and loving on her helped, but they both knew it was coming.

Miego reached for Yami, and once she was on his lap, his arms circled her body. He held her securely against him, planting kisses on her neck, face, and lips.

"This shit is on me. Don't cry, Yamiah. I did this shit, and I would do it all over again if I had to because he was a threat to you, and that was far more important to me than anything else. I know that's fucked up, but it's true. He didn't deserve you or baby girl, otherwise he would have been a better man. So I don't regret that shit, not even for a second, but it's fucking me up that a choice I made is hurting you and Ray."

"It's not about me, please don't think that. It's about Ray, I—"

"Yo, don't do that. You had a kid with that muthafucker, so I don't expect you not to feel some type away about it. I'm man enough to deal with that 'cause it don't take away from what I know you feel for me, but this ain't about that. I just need you to know, I'm sorry it hurt you and Ray, but I promise on everything I don't regret that shit and I never will."

He kissed her on the forehead and nudged her enough to stand. Once he was on his feet again, he wrapped Yami in his arms and kissed her gently on the lips.

"Imma go talk to her. Chill here for a minute."

Yami nodded, not knowing if it would help, but she decided to let him try. Anything that could possibly make Ray feel better was worth a shot, because right now, Ray saw her as the enemy.

Miego left Yami in the living room and headed down the hall to Ray's room. She was lying across the foot of her bed staring at the wall with her thumb in her mouth. He could tell that she had been crying. His heart was heavy, knowing that he was the reason behind it. It pissed him off even more that Black wasn't man enough to grow up and let Yami live her life so that he could still be here for her daughter.

"Hey, baby girl, what's wrong?" he asked after he lifted her tiny frame into his lap.

She let her head rest against his chest and snuggled closer to his body before her tiny voice filled the room.

"Mommy won't let me see my daddy," she whined.

"Come on, baby girl, you know your mom wouldn't do that. It's not that she won't let you see him, you just can't."

Miego looked up at Ray's doorway and Yami was standing in it, watching the two of them interact. Ray's back was to her, so she didn't see her mother standing there.

"Yes, I can. She just won't take me to my Nana's house. He'll come see me there."

Miego inhaled and let it out slowly. "No, Rayah, he can't. Your daddy can't come see you there either. He had to go away, and where he went, he can't come back."

"He can, he just has to drive there."

Miego smiled at how simple things were for her. At three years old, it was as simple as that, but in reality things were so much more complicated.

"You miss him?" Miego asked.

"Yesssss," Ray released with a pouty whine.

"He misses you too. He told me that if you ever missed him that you can close your eyes and feel his hugs and kisses, but he can't be here anymore, baby girl, and I'm sorry about that."

Yami smiled at Miego words. She knew how much he hated Black, but for Ray, he let that go enough to try and make things better for her.

"But I wanna see him." Ray's tiny voice was breaking him.

"I know, but how about this? If you promise not to cry or be mad at your mom, then we can go do something fun. Whatever you want, but you gotta promise not to cry anymore and you have to promise to go give your mommy a big hug and a kiss."

He waited, but Ray didn't say anything for a minute. The silence was killing Yami and Miego both, so when Ray finally answered, it created a sense of relief.

"Okay."

Miego tightened his hold on Ray and kissed her forehead again before he let her slip off his lap. She made a slow drag to the door where Yami was kneeling and waiting. When she reached her, Ray sluggishly fell into her mother's arms. The two hugged each other for a minute before Yami kissed her cheek and then smiled at her daughter.

"I love you, Ray."

"I love you too." Ray smiled before she planted another sloppy kiss on her mother's cheek.

"Can I watch TV now?" she asked with her eyes moving from her mother to Miego.

"Yep, go 'head," Yami said, running her hand across her daughter's head. After she was out of the room, Yami walked over to Miego and took Ray's spot.

"Thank you," she said with her hands on each side of his face. She pressed her lips against his.

Miego nodded and kissed her back a little deeper. He was still conflicted about the situation, but there wasn't anything he could do about it. For now, Ray was good, and that was enough for him to let it go.

Chapter Ten

"You smell really good for someone who's just going to hang with his boys," Yami said, partially playing but half serious as she sat on their bed watching Miego get dressed for his night out with Train and Memphis. Yanna, Yaz, and Lisa were coming over to chill at their apartment with her, which the guys used as an excuse to go to a party.

"I smell like I always smell, shorty. I didn't do anything different. The fuck you want me to do?"

He glanced over his shoulder before he entered their closet. She watched his sexy body, which was bare from the chest to the dark denim jeans that hung low around his waist, exposing the back elastic waistband of the boxer briefs that he wore.

"I want you to not smell good because I don't want those thirsty hoes all up on my man tonight," she yelled toward the closet, causing him to take one step out of it and grin at her.

"You jealous, Yamiah?"

She wanted to slap the smug grin off his face, but instead she just stuck her lips out into a pout. "Maybe. All that is for me and me only. You just remember that."

"You're tripping, can't no other female out there get shit from me and you know it."

"What I know is that you're a reformed hoe, and situations like what you're about to walk into tonight have a tendency to make people want to revisit those old ways. I would never know, right?"

Miego stepped into the closet again to find his shirt. Once he had it, he walked back into the closet and pulled it over his head.

"But I wouldn't. The fuck is that supposed to mean? No situation can control my actions. That shit is on me, and how the fuck you gon' call me hoe? You don't know shit about my past, shorty."

"Really?" Yami asked with her eyebrows raised, which made him laugh.

"Man, gone with that jealous shit. I ain't fucking with nobody but you. You know that, so kill all that, Yamiah, but I'm gon' be horny as fuck when I get home so be ready."

She laughed so deep, it made him laugh too. "You're so damn stupid. You're basically saying that you're gonna be around a bunch of bitches all night, which is gonna make you horny and then you wanna come home and lay up under me while you thinking about them. Saying some dumb shit like that, you better hope I'm here when you get back." Yami rolled her eyes before she peered at him.

Miego smiled and joined her on the bed, forcing her back and pinning her arms above her head before he began kissing and sucking on her neck. Just that alone had him instantly hard.

"Did I say shit about me being with you and thinking about some other bitch? You know better than that."

"And I know all about the party you're going to. I've been before, and I know they have strippers and half naked women there."

Miego kept kissing her body during their conversation, but after hearing that, he stopped long enough to look down at her with a cocky grin.

"I'm a man, so I'm not gon' sit here and lie to you and say that seeing that shit don't get my dick hard. The fuck you think? Just like you be 'bout to have a damn orgasm every time you see that little gay ass Michael Ealy on TV. But my point is, your pussy is the only one I wanna be inside, and the only one I'm gon' be inside for that matter. That's all you need to worry about. When I lay down with you, no other bitch is in my head 'cause I don't need that shit. This right here is enough. Trust that, shorty, now act like you don't know this dick belongs to you, and you gon' make me late proving it." Miego kissed her, and when he released it, she smiled.

"I swear you just can't help it can you?"

"Help what?"

"Saying whatever flows through your head."

Miego chuckled. "I could, but why the fuck would I? Take it or leave it. You know how I feel 'bout that shit."

He pecked her lips right before he got up again to finish getting ready. When he was done, he filled his pockets with money, his phone, and keys, right before Ray came running in the room. He grabbed her right before she was about to jump on the bed and held her in the air, causing her to giggle. Once he had her against his chest again, he kissed both her cheeks and she placed her small hands on the side of his face and pecked his lips.

"I need you to take care of your mommy for me tonight. Don't let her talk about me while I'm gone. Okay?"

Ray smiled. "I won't."

"And make sure you tell me everything they talk about while they're having this girl talk," he said playfully, frowning at her.

"I'm a girl too, so I can't."

"Aww, come on baby girl, you're supposed to be on my side." He pleaded with a pretend pout.

Ray looked at her mother and then back to him. "Nope, it's girls' night."

"Dang, it's like that?" Miego said with a slight chuckle.

Ray nodded and he kissed her cheek again before he lowered her to the bed, where she crawled over to her mother and climbed into her lap.

"That's all right, I still love you anyway," he said and winked at her just as the doorbell rang.

Ray climbed off the bed and ran to Miego, catching his hand just before he left the room. Yami shook her head at how quickly Ray had switched sides, but she was happy that her baby girl and Miego were so close.

Once they got to the door, Miego lifted Ray into his arms and let her check to monitor. "It's Aunty Yaz." She giggled so Miego proceeded to unlock the door and let them in.

"Hey mama." Yaz reached for Ray, pulling her out of Miego's arms. Once she had Ray secure, she kissed her niece and hugged her tightly.

"That's all you see, Yaz? Damn. You can at least throw me a head nod since you are entering my house," Miego teased, shoving her what he thought was just a little, but Yaz stumbled because he didn't know his own strength.

"You do see me holding Ray, don't you? Dumb ass," Yaz snapped before rolling her eyes and walking away to find her sister. Memphis walked in behind her and laughed before he and Miego dapped each other.

"You have patience like a muthafucker to be dealing with her annoying ass." Miego looked mad as hell for a brief second before he smiled.

He picked on Yaz all the time, but they were actually pretty tight now. Especially since their heart to heart about her situation with Memphis.

"Get off my shorty, bruh. I'm not gon' tell you that shit again."

"I guess you heard that?" Yaz said as she came back down the hall with Yami this time, instead of Ray.

Yami walked up to Memphis and hugged him before she slid her arm around Miego's waist.

"Man, fuck him, he can't tell me shit."

"Yeah, aight, keep thinking that shit, muthafucker." Memphis let his arm fall around Yaz, holding her against his body so that her back was to his chest. Once she was situated, he leaned down enough to kiss her neck.

"So should we be worried?" Yami asked, holding her head back to look up at Miego and then across at Memphis.

"Nah, you good. We're just chilling. Ain't shit fucking with what we got at home," Memphis said, and then kissed Yaz's neck again.

"I keep telling her that shit, but she so got damn paranoid." Miego grinned, looking down at Yami who sucked her teeth.

"I'm not paranoid. I just know what I have, and I'm not stupid. Commitment doesn't mean anything to trifling hoes," Yami said.

"Man, gone with that shit. It means something to me, and that's all you need to be worried about. Can't nobody get this dick if I ain't giving it. Trust that, shorty."

Memphis chuckled and shook his head. They were used to Miego, so none of them were affected by his statement.

"Yo, we need to head out so we can meet Train, though." He turned Yaz to face him. "Behave, don't be on that bullshit doggin' us out. I know how y'all get when you get together with your wine and shit." He playfully mugged Yaz and she shoved him in the chest.

"That's not what you need to worry about, you just worry about keeping those hoes out of your face tonight."

Memphis laughed and then shook his head. "I told you, you're good on that, shorty. Let that shit go."

The four of them said their goodbyes, and then Memphis and Miego left to meet Train, while Yami and Yaz got comfortable in the living room with snack trays and wine. Lisa and Yanna would be there soon, and Ray was situated in her room with movies and snacks of her own. The night had officially begun.

****

Lisa looked around Yami's living room grinning. It was late and she was way too tipsy. After the three of them shared four bottles of wine, she knew that there was no way she was going to make it home without some assistance. Tavion was asleep in Ray's room in the portable playpen she had brought with her, so the four of them were up alone, deep in conversation about their relationships.

"I'm drunk as shit," Yaz said before finishing off the last of the Moscato that was in her glass. It was so sweet and went down so smoothly, that she had damn near finished off a whole bottle by herself.

"So am I." Lisa giggled, holding her hand up like she was in a classroom.

"Why the hell you holding your hand up like that?" Yami asked before she burst out laughing.

"Shit if I know. I just did." Lisa said and giggled again. "I'm a bad parent. My son is in there asleep and I'm in here drunk." She frowned after looking over her shoulder toward the hallway that led to the bedrooms.

"No, you're not. He's fine, and we're not that drunk," Yami said, holding up her head, trying to appear confident.

"Yes, we are." Yaz laughed. "But he's good. We got him, and besides, he's sleep."

"You're right. I know I am, and I'm horny as hell too," Yami said.

"Too much info, boo. I really don't wanna hear all that right now." Yaz shook her head at her sister.

"Sorry, but it's true. I need my man to bring his ass home." She lifted her phone and pressed the button to check the time. She smiled at the picture of her, Miego, and Ray that was her lock screen.

"Your horny ass should have gotten some before he left then, with your nasty self. You know I did," Yaz said with a dazed look on her face as she remembered the events with her and Memphis from earlier.

"I did too, but that was forever ago," Yami said.

"I think I'm addicted to sex." Yanna blurted out, causing them all to look at her.

"Umm, okay, boo. Thank you for sharing," Yaz said and then giggled.

"Wait, so you did it? When?" Yami asked. The two of them had discussed it, but Yanna had never mentioned it again.

Yanna looked at Yami with a grin and nodded like a little kid. "I did, and a lot. That's why I think I'm addicted. It's like once I got started, I couldn't stop. I don't wanna stop."

"Her ass is definitely drunk," Lisa said, pointing at Yanna.

"I'm not drunk. I'm serious. I want it all the time, I think I need help." She pouted with a frown.

"Is it just Renz or other people?" Yami asked.

"Just Renz." Yanna's frown deepened.

"Girl, you don't need help. There's nothing wrong with being addicted to sex with your man. Good dick will do that to you, trust me. I can testify to that," Yaz said.

"Me too, oh lord, me too," Yami said, closing her eyes and thinking about it.

"First of all, eww, that's my brother. And second of all, it's the only dick I've ever had, so I don't know if it's good or not," Yanna said and then giggled.

"If you're talking about it, it's good, baby. Otherwise, it wouldn't even be on your mind," Yami said and then burst out laughing.

"Amen to that," Yaz said and high fived her sister.

"Well, it's been a minute for me, so I really need all of you to stop talking about it, please and thank you," Lisa said before mugging them all.

It had been a few days since she had been with Train, and since he was the only man that she was currently dealing with, she didn't really have any other options.

Lisa stood, stumbling just a little because her leg was asleep from having been tucked under her butt for so long. Once she regained her balance, she lifted the two empty bottles that were on the table in front of her and carried them and her glass into the kitchen.

"Train would kill me, I bet." After she placed bottles on the counter she pulled open the refrigerator and grabbed a bottle of water before returning to her seat.

"He's probably so much worse than you are right now, he can't say shit," Yami said with a scowl on her face, thinking about the fact that the guys were at a party without them, surrounded by an unlimited supply of liquor, drugs, and women.

She had talked to Miego a few times via text, but they were short. She tried not to let it bother her, but it did, a little.

"Yeah, but that's that double standard. They can do what they want, and we can do what they say," Lisa said with an annoyed expression.

"Girl, bye. Maybe you, but not me. I do what I want," Yaz said confidently.

"Really, now?" Yami questioned with a smug grin, looking at her sister.

"Yes, really. Memphis don't control me. I do what I want."

Lisa and Yami looked at each other and then giggled. "Mmhmm, let me see you tell him that. You forever telling me how I'm in check, but you're right there with me." Yami pointed at her sister.

"I'm forever telling you that because it's true, whether you believe it or not."

"Well, I, for one, don't really care what Train thinks. He's on a short string with me, and I have a feeling that we're about to be co-parenting anyway.

"Why you say that?" Yami asked.

She knew that Train wasn't the most faithful, but the few times that she had been around Lisa they seemed good. She assumed that was their deal, and whatever they had just worked. You would never guess that he was unfaithful, based on the way he treated her and their son. It was like she was the only woman in the world.

"You know why. He can't keep his dick in his pants, and I'm over that. I love him, but if he can't figure that out, then I'll be with someone who can," Lisa said with so much intensity that she even sat up to further make her point.

"Have you talked to him about that?" Yami asked.

She knew Train, and had heard him say a million times that Lisa wasn't going anywhere. She wondered if he had any idea where her head was at.

"Yep, more than enough times to give him fair warning, so that's on him if he wants to play dumb about it."

"He'll figure it out," Yami said, not knowing what else to say. She had been right where she was, and knew the feeling. She understood what it did to your heart to love someone who didn't love you enough to be what you needed.

Lisa shrugged. "He better, but either way, I'm still going to do what I need to do for me and Tavion.

The three ladies were quiet for a while as they processed. They all shared that in common, and it brought up a lot of emotions. Yami just prayed that Train figured it out because she was cool with Lisa, and hated the fact that she was having to deal with a situation like that.

Chapter Eleven

"Man, this shit is wild as fuck. They do this a lot?" Memphis asked, checking out his surroundings. The party they were at was live as hell, crowded as fuck, but everything seemed to be flowing smoothly so he was currently relaxed.

"Like twice a year. It's some wild ass shit. Dudes that usually be shooting at each other come to this shit and be passing blunts. I don't get it, but I ain't complaining," Miego said, looking around.

He was currently too high to really do anything but take up space on the sofa that he was sitting on. He had been there most of the night with the exception of the few times he checked out the area they had cleared out for the strippers. They were bad as hell, and he had spent more money on them than he should have, but it was all in fun. He wasn't fucking with any of them like that, even though a few of them that were now walking around damn near naked had pushed up on him.

He knew the game though. They were looking for a quick come up. They'd fuck him if that was what he wanted, but they were more interested in what was in his pockets versus his pants. That didn't faze him at all because he had no love for them in any way whatsoever.

Memphis chuckled before turning up the bottle he had in his hand. "This shit ain't nothing but trouble. Serious shit, my nigga."

"The devil's playground," Train said, looking around.

Unlike Memphis and Miego, he had slipped off a few times with a female or two, but he was currently chillin'. Unless he got a really good offer, he planned on heading to Lisa's house when he left there.

"Yo, look at Bank's big ass. Don't look like he give a fuck that his boy is gone. In fact, he looks happy as fuck." Miego nodded across the room toward were Black's homeboy was chilling, looking like he was having the time of his life.

"Man, fuck him. Weak ass muthafucker. He was Black's bitch anyway. Ain't no way I would have been letting anybody run me like that and still been fucking with him on some real shit. Hell yeah, that muthafucker is glad. He wasn't never gon' do shit on his own anyway.

Now he just stepped right into that muthafucker's place like it belonged to him all along," Train said.

Miego chuckled. "What the fuck you so mad about? You act like he took over our shit or something."

"I mean, really. You look like you ready to handle him or some shit like that," Memphis said.

"First of all, ain't no way he'd ever take shit from us, and I'm mad 'cause I hate a weak muthafucker. That shit just pisses me off. Man the fuck up and get your own. Don't be riding another man's dick," Train said.

"Yo, get his ass another drink. Calm the fuck down, bruh. You right, though, get your own. Don't be a bitch, kissing ass and taking orders to get shit done. He ain't shit. We could probably punk his bitch ass and take that muthafucker's territory. He better be glad we ain't fucking with those petty ass street sales around here anymore," Miego said.

"We could, though," Memphis said randomly.

"Could what?" Train asked after he realized what Memphis said.

"Take his shit. Why the fuck not? It ain't like he can stop us. I mean, I know you guys are doing your thing on a higher scale, but if we put the right people in place then you still don't have to touch shit. We can make that shit self-sufficient."

"Your ass sells guns. The fuck you know but pushing weight?" Miego said and chuckled. He already knew that was where Memphis got his start, so he was just fucking with him.

"Don't play me, bruh. You know I'm a man of many trades, so I know enough."

"Yo, he's right though. Us and them. That's all there is right now, why not make it just us? Shit, we already know you ain't going nowhere with your lying ass, so since we in it, let's really be in this shit. Ain't nothing wrong with getting a little closer to home."

Miego looked at Memphis and Train, who were both watching him and waiting. "Are y'all serious right now?"

"Fuck yeah. Does it look like I'm playing?" Memphis said.

"Shit, you already know me. I'm down for whatever."

"You know that shit is going to require us to handle a few people. Starting with him right there. You down for that? Shit just calmed down."

Memphis laughed. "Shit ain't never calm, but I'm wit it."

Train nodded. "Ain't nothing but a thang."

"Fuck, why do I feel like I'm gonna regret this shit?" Miego said with a big ass grin, knowing that he was about to co-sign.

"I guess we 'bout to get shit poppin', but tonight we're chillin'. We'll deal with that shit later," Train announced, holding out the bottle that was in his hand toward Memphis and then to Miego, who was still sitting on the sofa.

"You looked like you could use some company." A low budget female dressed in only a thong slid into Miego's lap and wrapped her arms around his neck. His head was back and his eyes were closed, so it caught him off guard. He quickly shoved her away from him, causing her to hit the floor.

"The fuck wrong with you? You don't know me like that shorty, damn."

She stood with a scowl on her face, which deepened when Train and Memphis both laughed.

"And you don't know me to be putting your hands on me." She raised her hand and leaned forward to slap him, but he caught her wrist and twisted her arm back before shoving her away from his body.

"Yo, you stupid as fuck. I was sitting here minding my got damn business before you brought your funky ass over here smelling like ten bad fucks, and you telling me not to put my hands on you. The fuck outta here with that bullshit, nasty ass. I should fuck you up for that shit."

Miego was on his feet, but Train stepped to him, making sure to get between the two. He knew that his boy was high as hell and drunk, and he already didn't have any filters. Miego to hurt her feelings in a way that was gonna cause her to need therapy to rebuild her self-esteem.

"Chill the fuck out, bruh, let her go."

"Man, fuck that bitch. Sitting her nasty ass on me, all dick infested and shit. She don't know me like that."

Train laughed and blocked Miego from getting around him, but focused on the girl. "Yo, you wrong as fuck for pushing up on him like that. You don't just get in people's personal space like that without permission, so you have to take what you get."

"That don't give him the right to put his hands on me," she yelled, still angry and embarrassed.

She had been watching him all night, and had waited until what she thought was the right time to approach him. Knowing that he was drunk, high, or both seemed like the perfect opportunity to fuck him and talk him outta of some cash. She knew exactly who he was.

"Bitch, if you don't get the fuck on with that shit. You better be glad I don't hit females or I'd knock your damn teeth out your fucking mouth."

Miego was mad as hell that she had invaded his personal space without permission, and then had the nerve to be mad at him. He didn't play about shit like that, and damn sure wasn't about to go home to Yami smelling like ass. He might have enjoyed the scenery, but he kept his distance. He wasn't down for disrespecting her like that.

"Yo, shorty, keep it moving. This ain't accomplishing shit," Train said.

"Fuck you, Miego. Trust me. You ain't all that."

Her statement made him laugh. "If I wasn't all that, you wouldn't have brought your nasty ass over here. Go find a dick to suck. The fuck outta here."

He found his place on the sofa again while she stood there glaring at him. Train was still between them and she knew it was pointless to say anything else, so she stormed off, cussing under her breath.

Memphis watched her leave and then looked at Miego and Train. "The fuck, yo? That shit was stupid funny. You didn't have to call her out like that though, bruh," he said and then chuckled.

"Fuck that hoe. Nasty ass. The fuck I look like having her all up on me like that when I got a shorty at home?"

"Yo, calm your hostile ass down. Here." Memphis lifted the blunt he had just rolled from the table in front of him and a brand new bottle of Hennessy then handed them both to Miego. "You need this shit more than me."

Miego looked up at him, still pissed, so it took him a minute but a smile crossed his face and he accepted what Memphis was handing him. "I guess I did go hard on shorty. She can't help that she's a nasty hoe. I shouldn't have called her out on that shit."

"The fuck? You're dumb as hell. I'm not fucking with you like that. How the hell you act like you feel bad, but then you still doggin' her ass out?"

Miego shrugged. "I ain't say I felt bad. The truth is the truth. I just don't wanna fuck up her hustle and have her in the bathroom crying and shit when she could be out here sucking dicks for stacks. I'm sure she got bills and shit." Miego's words flowed so natural, like what he was saying wasn't mean as hell.

"This muthafucker just don't give a fuck." Memphis laughed and walked back to the table he was sitting at, shaking his head. Train followed and the two of them continued talking and enjoying the environment while Miego went to work on the blunt Memphis gave him, followed by the bottle of Hennessy. After that, he was in a zone, and not worried about anything else.

****

"Look, Hope, he's lit. You should go empty his pockets since he snapped on you like he did."

Hope glanced at Miego and got pissed all over again about the way he had played her out earlier. She knew him and his reputation, so when she approached him, she thought for sure that she had hit the jackpot until he dissed her, and hard. When her girl, Amina, told her that he was off limits now because he was kicking it with Yami, it made things worse. She hated Yami because it seemed like every guy she ever wanted, Yami ended up with. It started in high school, and continued on after they graduated when Yami ended up pregnant by Black.

It wasn't like Yami was even actually stealing Hope's men, it just worked out that everybody Hope had her eye on, had their eye on Yami. She eyed Miego, noticing an iPhone in his hand and got another idea. She didn't want his money. Hope planned on fucking him over another way.

"Nah, I don't want his money. I wanna fuck up his happy little life," Hope said with a grin.

She looked around the party and noticed Train and Memphis across the room watching some girls strip. After realizing the coast was clear, she walked over to Miego and kissed the side of his face. He didn't budge, so she whispered his name in his ear, and he still didn't move. A grin spread across her face as she pulled her shirt over her head, exposing her bare breasts before she handed her girl her phone.

Amina looked at her strangely. "Girl, what you about to do?"

"You'll see. Take the picture for me." Hope moved slowly to him and straddled his lap. Once she was situated, she slid his phone out of his hand and touched the camera icon at the bottom.

Assuming he had a passcode on his phone, she knew that she could still take pictures with it. What she hoped was that Yami would go through it and find them. If he was like most guys, he didn't take pictures, so it could be days or even weeks before he realized the pictures were there. Even if he erased them, she would have the ones on her phone that she was about to have her girl, Amina take. Either way, she was about to complicate his life.

"Girl, if Miego finds out what you doing, he's gon' beat your ass. You do know who he is," Amina said with a grin, all too willing to help Hope out.

"He won't know. I'm not gon' have my face in the picture."

She turned her body, leaning forward seductively and placing her lips against his, while holding up his phone and taking a few shots. Amina did the same from where she was standing, and then Hope quickly got off his lap and tossed his phone on the sofa next to him. He was so out of it that he didn't move, not even once.

She grabbed her shirt and then the two of them made their way to the front of the party to leave. She was grinning the entire time, praying that her plan worked. If it did, he was going to have a lot of explaining to do courtesy of her, and the best part was that he would never know who set him up.

Chapter Twelve

"Can you turn that shit down, please? You're killing me, shorty." Miego lifted his head enough to open one eye and glance at Yami, who was in the kitchen blasting her Bose speaker with the playlist from her phone.

"You shouldn't drink if you can't handle your liquor," Yami said with a smirk before she walked over to her speaker and adjusted the volume, but only a little. She was cleaning the kitchen and needed her music.

"I can handle my liquor, it's all the other shit that I mixed with it that's got me all fucked up in the game."

"Wow. That makes me feel real good about what you were doing last night," Yami said with an attitude.

He didn't get in until four in the morning, and the only reason he was up now was because he promised to take Ray to his mom's house so Yamiah could study for finals in peace. Yami was grateful that it was almost over, and ready for summer break.

"Man, I told your little ass I didn't do shit last night but chill, so you can dead all that." He let his head fall back again, and his eyes were closed the second his head rested on the sofa again.

"Mommy, I wanna take a picture. Can I see your phone?" Ray said.

She ran into the kitchen and reached for her mother's phone, which was sitting on the counter. Yami snatched it up before she could get to it. She didn't want Ray to interrupt her music.

"No, Ray, I'm using mine right now."

"Mommy, please," Ray begged.

"Here you go, baby girl, you can use mine."

She ran over to him and was instantly happy again. He dug in his pocket, unlocked his phone and handed it over to her. The second it was in her small hands, she held it up, taking a few shots of herself making faces, before climbing in his lap and including him in a few more.

When she was satisfied, she jumped down and ran back to her mother, beaming at her work. Ray held the phone out for Yami to see. "Look, Mommy, look."

Yami took the phone from her and began scrolling through the pictures, smiling until she got to something that had her blood boiling. Miego only had eight pictures in his phone. The five that Ray had just taken, one that she took months ago of him, her and Ray, and then two of him with some half-dressed female straddling his lap, and they were kissing. She also noticed that he was in the clothes he wore last night.

"Ray, go to your room for a minute and let me talk to Miego."

"But, Mommy, I'm about to go to Nana GiGi's house."

"Ray, go to your room," Yami said, raising her voice just a little, which made Ray pout and Miego open his eyes again to see what was going on.

Ray took off running down the hall. Yami felt bad when she heard her door slam, but she couldn't worry about that right now. She'd deal with Ray in a minute, knowing that it would be easy to get back on her daughter's good side. Right now she needed to find out who the fuck was the female her so called man was kissing, and why that shit was in his phone.

"The fuck you yell at her like that for, Yamiah?" Miego asked, giving Yami the nastiest look.

Neither of them really did that. They were firm with her, but for the most part, Ray was a good kid so they never had a reason to yell at her. Yami doing it now didn't sit well with him.

"Don't worry about Ray. Worry about explaining the bitch you were kissing on last night," Yami yelled and threw his phone at him, which he caught just before it hit him in the chest.

"What the hell is wrong with you, shorty?"

"You are what's wrong with me. Look at your damn phone, Miego."

He glared at her for a minute, confused as hell before he looked down at his phone. The picture on the screen instantly had him heated. He knew it was from last night, but he didn't know who the fuck the girl was, why she had her lips on him, or how the fuck the picture of it was in his phone. It was clear from the angle that she took it, but you couldn't see her face. He knew that it must have been when he was passed out, but looking at the picture, it appeared that the two were kissing. That was some straight up bullshit because he damn sure knew he wasn't kissing anybody last night, not while he was conscious anyway.

"Hold up, shorty. I know this shit looks suspect as hell, but I promise you on everything, I don't know who the fuck this is. And it's damn sure not what you're thinking."

"Oh, so you don't want me to think that some bitch is on your lap, she doesn't have any clothes on, and your lips are on her. Because that's exactly what I'm thinking, but only because those are the facts. If you didn't want me to think that, then you should have been more careful with your got damn phone, asshole."

"Yo, you need to calm that shit down. I'm telling you I wasn't kissing that bitch. In fact, I don't even know who that is."

He was wracking his brain trying to remember the events of last night. Everything in him was telling him that he didn't do shit, but there was a considerable amount of time when he was so lit that he passed out. It was possible that he could have done something that he didn't remember doing, but it just didn't feel right. It felt like bullshit.

"Well, apparently she knows you, and she knows you pretty damn well. How the fuck did she get your phone, Miego? And why does the bitch have her lips on you?"

"Shit, the fuck if I know. I was high as hell last night, and I drank so much I can't even tell you what happened. But I know I didn't cheat on you, shorty. I'd bet my life on that. She might have done that shit while I was out, but I damn sure wasn't aware of it, and I know I didn't fuck that bitch, so get that shit out your head."

Yami laughed sarcastically. "You just told me you don't know what you did, so how can you bet your life on that? You sound dumb as fuck right now. You might have fucked every bitch in there, and just don't remember."

"Yamiah, really?" Miego stood there looking at her like she had lost her mind. For him it was so simple. He said he didn't do it so, she needed to believe him. Why the hell couldn't she just believe him?

"You know what, don't worry about it. You're right, I'm just crazy." She turned and started cleaning the kitchen again, throwing dishes in the sink and slamming cabinets and drawers.

Miego just stood there and watched, frustrated as hell, trying to figure out what to say to get this situation under control. He wasn't used to shit like this.

It wasn't like he ever cared enough about any female's feelings to explain his actions, false or not. If this had been anybody but Yamiah, he would have just said fuck it and walked away. Because it was her, it had him frustrated as hell. The idea that she thought he would cheat pissed him off, and knowing that she was hurting because she actually believed he did, had him feeling like shit. That was the worst part. He was feeling bad about some shit that he knew he didn't do.

After a few minutes, he walked over to her, and when he was close enough, he enclosed her body with his arms, holding her against his chest. She tired her best to fight him off, but her arms were pinned to her side and he was a lot stronger than she was. Being that close to him made her weak, and she didn't want to let her heart force her to make a stupid decision like believing in him, when the facts were right in front of her face.

"Yamiah, chill for a minute and just listen to me."

"I told you I'm good. You didn't do shit, and I'm just crazy," she snapped sarcastically.

"Shorty, don't do that shit. It's so easy for you to just believe the worst, but will you at least consider that it's not what you think?"

"If it's not, how the fuck did she get your phone, and how would you not know that she was on you like that unless you wanted her to be?"

"Man, you know bitches be doing any and everything to fuck up a good thing. I bet she was counting on you seeing that shit. I damn sure didn't give her my phone, but as much as Ray be in your shit, you know she could have easily gone to my camera without having my password. I don't use that shit, so I would have never known the damn picture was in there. Can you just consider the fact that it's not what it looks like?"

"But you don't even know for sure, so why would you expect me to believe it's anything other than what I see? You just told me you don't remember what you did. Maybe you were with her and just don't remember. Either way, I just can't deal with that right now, so please let me go."

Miego held onto her for a few moments more before he released a sigh, kissed her on the temple and then stepped back.

"Can we leave now?" Ray's whiny voice made Yami and Miego both turn to face her.

"Yeah, let me get my keys, baby girl."

"No, she's not going," Yami said, frowning at him.

"Don't do that shit, Yamiah. Don't punish her because you're mad at me. This don't have shit to do with her," Miego said, looking her right in her eyes before he turned to Ray. "Go get your bag, Ray."

Ray followed his instructions and took off down the hall. Miego followed but went to their bedroom and the two of them returned a few minutes later, Ray with her bag, and Miego holding his keys.

Yami didn't really want to let her daughter go, but he was right, there was no point in punishing her because she was mad at him. She knew that his mother would be heartbroken if she kept Ray away from her. Besides, Yami already felt bad for yelling at Ray, so she decided to let it go.

"Give me a hug, Ray," Yami said, kneeling down and holding her arms open.

Ray hesitated for a minute, but she ran to her mother and fell into her embrace.

"Be good, okay, and I'll see you tomorrow. I'll call you before you go to sleep."

"Okay, I love you." Ray said, grinning at her mother. She got what she wanted, so she was happy again.

"Love you more." Yami hugged her daughter one last time before she ran up to Miego and took his hand.

She watched as the two of them made it to the door and then were gone. She was so furious and hurt that she didn't know what to do with herself, but she knew for sure that she wouldn't be studying for her mind terms like she originally planned.

The entire drive to his mother's house, Ray talked his ear off and he tried his best to keep his attitude under wraps, but he was fuming. Even though he was pissed with Yami for not believing him, he couldn't really be mad at her. Hell, if the situation were reversed, he would have reacted the same way. Right now, he needed to figure out a way to fix it.

After he pulled up in front of his mother's building, he parked, got out, and moved to the back door to get Ray. She was in the process of unbuckling herself from her car seat before he even got to her, which had him smiling. She was so independent sometimes, and he loved that about her. He was going to make sure she had every advantage to be anything she wanted to be.

"Let's go, baby girl. I see you don't need me." He smiled at her when he had the car door open, and reached in to lift her out of her car seat.

Once she was in his arms, she threw her arms around his neck and pressed her face against his with a giggle. "I need you, and so does Mommy."

"Word, how is that?" he asked, unable to contain his smile as they made their way through his mother's building.

"Because you take care of us," she said, like it was so simple. But it meant everything in the world.

"You take care of me too," he responded as they stood in front of his mother's door, waiting while he fumbled with the keys to unlock it.

"I can do it. My daddy used to let me open his door," Ray said, reaching for Miego's keys.

Hearing her talk about Black hit him hard, but at least she wasn't upset, so he held out the key and positioned her so that she could reach the lock. He guided her hand and helped her as much as she would let him, but of course she wanted to do it on her own.

"Did I give you keys to my house, pretty girl?" Ginette said as soon as Ray had the door unlocked and opened.

"No, he did." Ray giggled and ran to jump into Ginette's arms.

Ginette lifted her from the floor and hugged her tight before delivering a series of kisses. "I guess that's okay, then," she said before letting Ray slide down her body.

"Sup, old lady?" Miego said as he hugged his mother and kissed her on the cheek.

"Call me old again and you'll see. You staying for a minute?"

"Nah, I have a few things to do before I head home."

"Okay, tell Yamiah I said I'll call her later."

"I'm not telling her shit," Miego said pulling his phone out when it went off with a notification. He hoped it was Yamiah, but he knew better.

"Mommy's mad at him," Ray said, before she skipped down the hall to meet Yanna, who was heading her way. Ginette frowned at her son, which made him shake his head. The last thing he wanted was for her to be all in his business, because he knew that she would take Yamiah's side.

"What did you do?" Yanna asked when she was close enough to punch in him in the arm.

Ray was now on the sofa with the remote in her hands.

"I didn't do shit, she just thinks I did."

"Well, what did you do to make her think you did something?" Ginette asked.

"I was at a party last night and—"

"You went to that? You shouldn't have been there in the first place. I would be mad at your dumb ass too," Yanna said, which caused her mother to give her a warning look about her language.

"Man, chill, I didn't do shit. But at some point, I blacked out and some chick got my phone and took pictures of us."

"Doing what?" Yanna asked.

Ginette waved her hand in the air. "I don't even want to hear this. Just fix it. That child has enough issues without you adding to it by doing stupid stuff." She pointed at her son and then gave him a stern look before turning to Ray. "Come on, Ray, let's go make some cupcakes."

Ray jumped up and ran to her. Miego grabbed her and lifted her in the air. "Give me a kiss, baby girl, and I'll see you tomorrow."

He hugged Ray and she pecked his cheek before he lowered her to the floor again and she disappeared into the kitchen with his mother.

"Let me see the pictures," Yanna said, holding out her hand for her brother to hand over his pone.

He unlocked the phone and scrolled through the pictures before handing the phone over. The second she laid eyes on them he she balled up her fist and punched him as hard as she could.

"You better be glad that she's just mad and didn't leave your stupid ass. This looks bad. Who the hell is she, Miego? You had sex with this girl, didn't you?"

"Hell no, the fuck outta here with that. I don't know who she is. I don't even remember that shit. I was high as fuck, and drank two bottles of Hennessy. I passed out for a minute, but I know I didn't fuck her."

"How you know that if you were out? You shouldn't have had your ass there in the first place. What did she say?"

"You know what she said, same shit you're saying. Damn, why can't y'all just believe I didn't do shit?" he said, frustrated.

"'Cause this says you did. Why would she believe anything else?" Yanna held up his phone.

"Give me my damn phone, I'm 'bout to find this hoe and she's gonna tell Yami the truth."

Yanna laughed. "You really think that makes sense? First of all, you don't even know who it is, and second of all, how you think you're gonna make her go to your girl and tell her the truth? What if the truth is that you fucked her and don't remember, then what?"

He stood there thinking about it for a minute. She was right, but that was a chance he had to take. "I know I didn't, and trust me, I'll make that bitch tell the truth. She don't wanna play with me."

"She already did," Yanna said with a smirk

"Kiss my ass. I'm out. I got shit to do."

"Miego, don't hurt that damn girl."

"I won't, if she tells the truth. Otherwise, all bets are off."

"I'm not even gonna say anything about that. I'll let you have it."

"Good, 'cause you know it wasn't gon' stop me anyway."

He winked at his sister before heading to the door. His first stop would be to Train's house to find out what the hell happened last night, and then from there, he had to find out who the hell the bitch was that was disrupting his life.

Chapter Thirteen

"What are you doing here?" Yaz asked when she opened her door and found her sister standing there.

"Damn, can I come see you, Yaz?" Yami said and pushed past her sister, making contact with her shoulder as she entered her apartment.

She looked around and smiled because things were so different. Her sister always had nice things, but on a budget. Right now, looking at the inside of her apartment, everything in it had Memphis written all over it. Yaz's voice put an end to her admiration of what had changed since her last visit.

"Not when you just show up, and carrying a bag like you're not going home. What's up, Yamiah?"

"I think Miego is cheating, or rather cheated on me." She dropped her bag on the floor next to her sister's sofa before falling back into it.

Yaz moved to Yami, but stopped in front of her with her arms folded, peering at her sister.

"Cheated or cheating? There's a difference. And what even makes you think that he did either?"

"I don't think, I know. It happened last night, and I found the picture of him with some trick on his lap, naked with her lips on his. I'd call that cheating."

"What did he have to say about it?"

"What do you think he said? He denied it, saying he didn't know how she got his phone and that he didn't cheat on me. He claims he doesn't even know her or how she ended up on him last night."

"It could be true, Yamiah. You know bitches forever pulling some slick shit, and Memphis did tell me that Miego was out of it for a while."

"Really, Yaz? Since when did you start defending him?"

"I'm not defending him, Yamiah, but that man treats you like a precious metal. You and Ray both, so why would he go out and do something dumb like that? I know I had my doubts about him, but not anymore. He's one of the good ones, boo."

"So good people don't fuck up? Would you be so quick to make excuses if you saw that in Memphis' phone?"

"Yes, good people fuck up. I'm not saying that, but just don't go writing him off as a cheater until you know for sure. I don't know what I would do, but right now this is about you and Miego. Where is he anyway, and where is Ray?"

"I don't know where he is and I don't really care. I'm not in the mood to deal with him right now so I came here and Ray is with his mom."

Yaz looked at her sister and laughed. "Your daughter is with his mother, but you're sitting here talking about you need some space. Girl, bye. If you really thought he was cheating, you'd be over him, and Rayah would be sitting right here with you."

"Shut up, it's not fair to disrupt her life because he can't keep his dick in his pants. If it's true, then I'll have to, because I refuse to be with a cheater. For now, I just need a minute. Can I get that, or nah?"

"You're grown, you can do whatever you want." Yaz chuckled and then left her sister to head to the kitchen.

"I'm staying here tonight," Yami yelled.

"Mmhmm, we'll see if he lets that happen."

"He doesn't have a choice."

"Yep," Yaz said and then laughed.

Yami didn't bother acknowledging her sister's sarcasm. She just dug through her purse and got her phone out. She didn't have any messages or missed calls, which annoyed her a little. For him to be so innocent, he damn sure wasn't trying to convince her. He just left to take Ray and now was out doing God knows what. Hell, he could be seeing the trick he was with last night for all she knew. Either way, she had no plans on going home tonight.

****

Miego stood outside of Train's door beating on it like he was 5-0. He knew Train was going be pissed, but fuck it, he was too. He needed to figure out what the hell happened last night. This whole situation was bullshit, and he was ready to be done with it. Problem was, he needed some help to make that happen. He figured after Yamiah calmed down, he could talk some sense into her and likely even get her to the point where she might believe him. That wasn't good enough because he knew it would always be in the back of her mind.

Every time he left the house or picked up his phone, she would be questioning his actions and motives, and he wasn't about to deal with that. The only way that wasn't gonna happen was to find out who the fuck the girl was, and force her to tell Yami the truth. Hell, she might not even believe that, but it was better than no explanation at all.

"Why the fuck you banging on my door like you got warrants for me and shit, Miego?" Train yelled when he made it to his door.

Miego pushed past him and waited for Train to close and lock the door.

"Yo, what the fuck happened last night?" Miego asked, mugging Train hard as hell. He hadn't even realized that Rich was in the room until he spoke up.

"Who the fuck pissed your ass off, and when is the funeral?" Rich said and chuckled.

"You were lit like a muthafucker is what the fuck happened. What's up? Sis mad cause your ass didn't get in until four this morning?"

"Nah, she mad 'cause some bitch got my phone and took pictures of herself on my lap with her nasty ass lips on me."

"Yo, stop playing." Train laughed until he realized Miego was serious.

"Shut the fuck up, you're serious?"

Miego pulled his phone out and went to the pictures. Once he had it up, he passed his phone to Train. Rich stood behind him looking also as they examined the pictures.

"When the fuck did this shit happen?" Train asked.

"I don't know, that's why I'm here asking you."

"Yo, I know her. That's Hope," Rich said.

"How you know?" Miego asked.

"That tattoo on her back. She works down at Eye Candy, I bet she's there now."

Miego snatched his phone from Train and pointed to Rich. "Let's go."

"Where the fuck we going?" Rich asked. Train was curious too, so he waited.

"I'm 'bout to go get that bitch, she gon' tell Yamiah the truth or Imma send Yanna down there to fuck her up."

"You can't just go get that hoe. And what makes you think she gon' tell the truth, especially to your girl?" Train asked.

"Trust me, I'm a problem she don't want. She gon' tell the truth. Let's go."

Train laughed. "You dumb as fuck, but I'm with it. Only because I can't wait to see how this shit 'bout to play out."

Not long after, the three of them were inside Eye Candy looking around. It was a low budget joint, so it wasn't crowded at all. Miego was pissed because they had to pay to get in, which made his attitude worse. Hope was definitely about to have a problem on her hands.

After looking around and no sight of her anywhere, Miego grabbed the first girl he saw by the arm and yanked her toward him. "Yo, you know Hope?"

"Can you get your hands off me, please?" she snapped, yanking away from him with a scowl on her face.

"Can you answer my got damn question? I don't want your raggedy ass, and I ain't gon' do shit to you."

Train chuckled and took over, knowing that they weren't going to get anywhere dealing with his bipolar ass.

"He didn't mean nothing by it, baby girl—"

"Yes, the fuck I did. I'm serious as a muthafucker," Miego said, cutting him off and grilling her hard as hell.

"Shut the fuck up." Train said, pointing at Miego. "Like I was saying, we're looking for Hope. Can you help me out?"

"You're looking for Hope or he's looking for Hope?" She narrowed her eyes at Miego and then focused on Train again.

Train gave Miego a look that told him to keep his mouth shut before he answered. "I am." He reached in his pocket and pulled out a few bills and held them up."

She took them from him and then smiled. "She's up next. Should be on stage in a minute," she delivered before winking at Train and walking off.

"You owe me two bills," Train said, pointing at Miego.

"I don't owe you shit," he said and laughed. "I didn't tell you to give her dusty ass money."

"You wanted to know where Hope was, and now we do. You owe me."

Rich laughed. "Both of y'all need help. I swear ain't neither one of you right."

"That's him." Train and Miego both said at the same time and then grilled each other.

"Yo, let's go."

"Where?"

"Down there." Miego pointed to the stage and started moving.

"The fuck you gon' do, snatch her ass off the stage?" Train asked Miego, only half playing.

"Hell yeah, and then she's going with us."

"You can't just snatch her ass off the stage, Miego, damn," Rich said laughing.

"Who gon' stop me?"

The music started just as they reached the stage and then the announcer called out her name. Miego stood right in front of it with his arms folded and waited. Sure enough, Hope walked out and grabbed the pole, doing her thing.

"Yo, isn't that old girl from the party? The one you embarrassed about stepping to you?" Train pointed to Hope, tilting his head to the side to get a better look.

"Hell yeah. She got me fucked up, but I got something for that." After realizing who she was, Miego got amped as hell and was ready to get his hands on her.

"Wait so, she set your ass up because you embarrassed her last night?" Rich asked, looking from Train to Miego.

"You know this muthafucker don't know how to talk to anybody. He went in on her ass, damn near had her in tears, so this shit is his fault." Train laughed nodding at Miego who was on the verge of knocking both of them out.

"I hate I missed that. This fool don't have no damn sense, so I know that shit was funny as hell." Rick grinned at Miego, not moved by the fact that he was annoyed with him and Train both.

"Yo, both y'all can shut the fuck up and let's do this shit." Miego yelled, moving closer to the stage.

Hope was so caught up in her performance that she hadn't even realized that the three of them were right there watching her, but it didn't last long because she was taken by surprise when Miego reached up, grabbed her ankle and yanked the shit out of it.

She landed on her butt and looked around shocked until she laid eyes on him, causing fear to set in. To say she was scared wouldn't even touch how she was feeling. Her eyes bucked wide as hell, and she scrambled, trying to get back, but couldn't because of the tight grip he had on her ankle. Panic set in, so she started violently kicking with her free leg. Her heel caught the side of Miego's face, which really pissed him off.

Furious, he grabbed her other leg and yanked both of them so hard that she hit the floor in front of the stage. She had definitely fucked with the wrong person, and he was about to make that clear.

She struggled to get on her feet, but he grabbed her arm to hold her in place.

"Heads up, yo," Train said when he noticed security coming toward them.

"What the fuck are you doing here?" Hope yelled after she was upright.

Ignoring her, Miego pulled her close and whispered in her ear, "If you don't want to die today, tell them you're good and to go the fuck away."

"I'm not telling them shit," she yelled.

Miego chuckled and then lifted his shirt to expose his gun. He wasn't going to shoot her, but she damn sure didn't know that.

"Tell them you're good, shorty."

"What's going on up here, Hope?"

Miego looked at the security guard and smiled. He was a big guy, looking like the body builder type, but that didn't mean shit to him. He'd still beat his ass, and with Train and Rich backing him up, it was best that this dude kept it moving.

Miego tightened his grip on Hope's arm, forcing her to speak up. "I'm good, just a misunderstanding."

"Don't look like you're good. If something's going on, I can handle it for you, Hope."

"Nah, she's good. Like she said, just a misunderstanding," Miego said, looking him right in the eye with a smirk on his face. He really wanted dude to try him.

"Hope, you sure?" he asked, ignoring Miego and looking at her.

"I'm sure. Everything's fine.'

"Let's go." Miego said, damn near dragging her.

She cooperated, not knowing what to expect. If he was crazy enough to show up at her job and yank her off the stage, then there was no telling what he might do, and she wasn't about to die today.

The security guard watched as they made their way toward the entrance of the building, but elected not to get involved. The girls that worked there always had one issue or another, and he had been instructed by the club's owner not to get involved unless the girls specifically asked him to. In the past, they had tried to handle things, and then some of the women had gone back and turned on them for stepping up. So, for now, if it didn't appear that there was any immediate danger, they keep their distance.

"Where are you taking me?" Hope yelled, trying to decide what her next move would be.

The look Miego gave her had her heart racing. "You're 'bout to go tell my girl that I didn't fuck you last night."

"Yo, Rich, ride back there with her dumb ass so that she don't jump out or no shit like that."

"She ain't 'bout to jump out a moving car, yo."

"Shit, you never know. This bitch sneaky as fuck, and she ain't too damn bright. Give her your shirt. I can't take her nasty ass to Yami looking like that."

"Hell no, the fuck?"

"Man, give her that one. I'll buy you another one, damn." Miego said, pointing to the button up that Rich had over the pocket tee that he was wearing.

He looked at Miego like he had lost his mind, until Train spoke up.

"Just give her the damn shirt so we can get this shit over with."

"Can I go get my purse and my phone please? I promise, I'll go, but I—"

"Hell no, you don't need that shit. Get in the got damn car and your ass better be clean or Imma fuck you up. I swear, you better not have my leather smelling like ass," Miego said, pulling his door open and getting in.

Train just shook his head and did the same. Rich waited for Hope to get in and then followed. There was no point in arguing with him because he wasn't trying to hear shit that either of them were saying right now. His only goal was getting Hope to Yami so that she could tell her what really went down last night.

Chapter Fourteen

Miego returned to his car, got in and slammed the door. Train looked at him like he was crazy, trying to figure out what his problem was, but Miego pulled his phone out and was on it before he could say anything to him, so instead he listened and waited.

"Yo, where the fuck is she? Man, don't fucking play. I just left our apartment and she ain't there, so I know you know where she is, Yaz. Man, chill with all that. I'm 'bout to fix that shit right now. I'm on my way, don't tell her I'm coming. Your simple ass owes me anyway, so don't tell her, Yaz."

Train shook his head and laughed as he watched Miego drop his phone in his lap and start his car again.

"How the fuck you gon' ask her to do you a solid and then call her simple? You know she gon' tell sis you're heading that way, right?"

"She better not. Yaz know I don't mean nothing by that shit."

Miego pulled off, looking in his rearview, and caught a glimpse of Hope who was looking right back at him. She was mad as hell, but he didn't really care. She should have minded her damn business, and she wouldn't be in this shit and neither would he.

It took them another forty minutes to get to Yaz's apartment, and none of them really said much. Train and Rich smoked while Hope sat in the back with her lips poked out and arms folded.

"Yo, get that bitch out the car and let's go," Miego tossed over his shoulder before he got out and stepped onto the sidewalk, followed by Train.

"I'm not a bitch, and you don't have to be so rude."

Miego stopped dead in his tracks and looked at Hope with murderous eyes. "You obviously ain't too damn bright, so let me make this shit real simple for you. Keep your fucking mouth closed until I tell you to speak, 'cause you getting real close to me fucking your dumb ass up on some real shit."

Rich laughed, grabbed her arm, and followed Miego and Train, dragging Hope with him. He thought the whole thing was funny as hell, and he couldn't wait to see how it was about to play out.

Once they reached Yaz's door, Miego pounded on it so hard that two neighbors opened their doors to see what was going on, which pissed him off even more because they were being nosey.

Yaz pulled the door open, giving him a death stare, but Miego ignored her, grabbed Hope and dragged her with him as he pushed past Yaz.

"Where she at?"

"The fuck you mean, where she at? The more important question is why the hell you brought this trash to my house?" Yaz pointed at Hope but kept her eye on Miego.

"Ain't gon' be too many more times for you to call me trash, hoe." Hope said, pointing back at Yaz while Miego still had a hold on her arm.

It was clear from the way Yaz reacted that she knew Hope, and he didn't need anything to pop off before Hope cleared things up with Yami. After that, he didn't care what happened.

"Man, Yaz, get your sister, and you shut the fuck up."

"What's going on?" Yami asked, walking down the hall with her arms folded.

She had heard Miego's voice and her sister yelling, but the second she laid eyes on Hope, she felt a rush of anger flow through her body. The fact that Miego had her by the arm wasn't helping things.

"And here we go," Train said with a smirk before he got comfortable on Yaz's sofa, followed by Rich.

"Tell her what your stupid ass did," Miego demanded, shoving Hope toward Yami.

If looks could kill, both Miego and Hope's families would be preparing for some services.

"She don't need to tell me shit, but you do. Why the fuck is she here, and dressed like she just climbed out of someone's bed?"

"She's here cause your stubborn ass didn't wanna believe me, so just listen to what the fuck she has to say."

"Why would I listen to this bitch? She ain't shit. Never been shit, and ain't gon' be shit." Yami released her words and made sure she kept her eyes on Hope in a way that dared her to say something.

Yami's eyes were all over Hope, who was wearing Rich's plaid button up. It was open, exposing a thong and bra set. She didn't have a clue what was going on, but whatever it was had her pissed.

"Shorty, just listen to this bitch, she's about to clear that shit up right now," Miego said, getting frustrated.

He looked down at Hope and she rolled her eyes, but knew better than to keep playing with her life by not doing what he asked.

"He didn't cheat on you," she released with more attitude than either Yami or Yaz was willing to deal with.

"Nah shorty, tell the whole story, my nigga," Miego said, pointing at Hope.

"He didn't know what I was doing. I took his phone and—"

Before she could finish, Yami rushed Hope and punched her dead in her face, but didn't stop there. Hope was about a foot taller than her, but couldn't really defend herself because Yami was going at her so hard. Seeing her sister in action prompted Yaz to jump in. The two of them beat the brakes off Hope, to the point where she was balled up on the floor covering her head with her arms, in an attempt to shield her face from the two of them.

"Bruh, get sis. She fucking shorty up," Train said through a laugh, after it got to be too much. He jumped up, grabbed Yaz around the waist, and yanked her off Hope, which only left Yami to deliver her ass whooping.

"I ain't doing shit. Her dumb ass should've known better than to fuck with me and my shorty. She need her ass whooped.

"Train, let me go or Imma fuck you up too," Yaz yelled, trying her best to break free of the hold he had on her.

"That shit ain't gon' happen, but chill the fuck out yo, y'all already fucked her up. Miego, stop playing and get Yami before we fuck around and have a body on our hands."

Miego chuckled at the sight of Yami going ham on Hope, but decided it was enough. He grabbed her and tried to lift her in the air, but she had a fist full of Hope's hair and Hope came up with her."

"Yamiah, let her ass go, damn shorty. You gon' make that bitch bald headed."

"Fuck her," Yami yelled before kicking the shit out of Hope and releasing her hair at the same time, causing Hope to hit the floor and back away from the two of them.

"You people are crazy!" Hope yelled when she was finally able to get on her feet again. Her eye was swelling shut and she had multiple bruises on her face. Her hair was all over her head while she tried to cover her body with Rich's shirt.

"Bitch, you haven't seen crazy. You petty as fuck for that shit you pulled. If I didn't know any better, I'd swear your ass was still in high school. You been hating on my sister since then. It must be a sad fucking life to be holding on to that shit," Yaz yelled, once again trying to break free of Train.

"I'm not holding on to anything. Ain't no body worried about your damn sister," Hope said, trying her best to regain some type of respect. She knew she looked bad.

Yami laughed sarcastically. "You ain't worried about me, but you chasing after my man on some petty bullshit? Get the fuck outta here with that."

"Fuck you and him," Hope yelled, feeling stupid as she glared at Yami.

"Bitch, you tried that, but I see he turned your ass down. As for me, you ain't my type, boo," Yami said with a smirk and blew Hope a kiss.

Miego laughed, turned on by how hard Yami was going. He had never seen that side of her, and he actually liked it. He wasn't the type for females fighting on some hood type shit, but Hope had it coming. Now that it was over, he was about to get with Yami about not believing him.

"Man, get this bitch outta here." He nodded to Rich, who was sitting calmly, taking in the whole scene. It was funny as hell to him, so he just sat back and watched.

"What you want me to do with her?" he asked, looking Miego's way with raised eyebrows. They had brought her there in Miego's car, and Rich damn sure wasn't about to take her anywhere.

"I don't give a fuck, just get her outta here. Leave her ass in the hallway for all I care. I'm done, she served her purpose."

"You're going to take me back to the club, aren't you?" Hope looked right at Miego with pleading eyes.

She knew that he didn't owe her anything, but she had done what he asked and got her ass beat in the process. She also didn't have her purse or phone.

"Fuck no, your ass can walk."

"I don't have my purse or my phone. How the hell am I supposed to get back?"

"Give that hoe money for the bus," Yami said with a grin.

"Hell no, she ain't getting shit from me," Miego said.

Train sighed before he reached in his pocket. He held Yaz with one arm and used his free one to hand Hope a twenty.

"Yo, take this shit, shorty, but I suggest you get the fuck outta here and fast, 'cause I'm 'bout to let Yaz go. If she catch your ass, I'm not gon' stop her this time."

Rich chuckled and grabbed Hope's arm then pulled her to the door. She snatched the twenty from Train and walked out.

Miego lifted Yami off her feet and took her down the hall to Yaz's bathroom. Once they were inside, he slammed and locked the door.

"You happy now? I told your paranoid ass that I didn't cheat on you," he said after he put Yami down and stood in front of the door to block it.

She folded her arms and grilled him, but didn't say anything because she didn't really have anything to say. At this point, she knew she was wrong for not believing him, but it wasn't her fault. What else was she supposed to think after seeing those pictures?

"Oh, you can't say shit now? You had a lot to say before, but now that you know that shit ain't true, you can't fucking talk?" Miego yelled.

"So you didn't cheat, and what? You shouldn't have been there in the first place and it would have never happened."

Miego chuckled. "You so damn stubborn. You wrong as fuck right now, and you still trying put that shit on me. What the fuck am I supposed to do, shorty? Sit up under your little ass twenty-four seven, huh? I can't go out? We both know that shit ain't gon' work, but what is gon' work is the fact that you need to trust me."

He stepped to her and grabbed her by the belt loops of her jeans with one hand while he used the other to start unfastening them.

"It's not about you going out. It's about what you do while you're out."

"I didn't do shit, she just told you that, and you need to trust me. How many times I gotta tell you that this dick don't belong to nobody but you." He used his hands to push her jeans and panties down her hips while keeping eye contact with her. "Take them off, shorty," he said as he began to unbuckle his jeans.

Yami did as instructed and stepped out of hers.

"You gon' trust me from now on?" Miego asked, lifting her onto the counter and then kissing her on the neck first before connecting with her lips.

She nodded, but didn't speak.

"Nah shorty, say that shit. I need to hear it," he said, pulling her hips toward him to the point that he had to hold her up so that she wouldn't fall.

Just as she opened her mouth to speak, he positioned himself at her opening and forced his way inside her so roughly that she gasped for air and threw her head back.

"Tell me, Yamiah," he said, pulling out of her slowly and then forcefully pushing into her again, so that their pelvises were connected.

She took a deep breath before placing her hands on the counter behind her to brace herself. "I trust you."

Her eyes were closed tight as she enjoyed the feel of him inside her. She felt like he was trying to kill her with the way he entered her so roughly, but she damn sure wasn't about to complain.

"Look at me, Yamiah." Miego's voice forced her eyes open and they met with his. He had such an intense look on his face that it scared her a little.

"Don't doubt me, shorty. I ain't fucking with nobody but you, and I put that on everything. I need you to always believe me over anybody else, even when things seem like they could be some bullshit."

Yami bit down on her lip and nodded. His strokes were so deep that she felt her orgasm building, and she couldn't speak. Instead, she just closed her eyes again and threw her head back. Miego smirked, knowing that she was about it cum. He was right there with her, and after a few more deep strokes, he pulled her against his chest and released everything he had in him. Neither of them moved for what felt like forever until someone started beating on the door.

"You in there fucking and I'm ready to go. Bring your ass on," Train yelled from the other side of the door, which made Yami and Miego look at each other and laugh.

"Hold the fuck up, I'm coming, damn," Miego yelled back before he stepped away from Yami slowly because he was still sensitive.

He lifted her from the counter, and after the two got themselves cleaned up and dressed again, he sat on the edge of the tub and pulled her into his lap.

"You know that shit was sexy as hell the way you fucked her up, but don't think that shit is cool, though. I don't want you fighting like that. Especially not if has something to do with me. You never have to fight another bitch over me, 'cause I promise, I'm all yours. So stop doubting that shit, aight?"

"Can you blame me, though? You would have been the same way."

Miego chuckled. "You're right, but wouldn't have been no fighting, shorty, just bullets flying. I need you to trust me. I know that's a lot to ask, especially since you're used to muthafuckers being on some fuck shit with you, but that ain't me, Yamiah, and I think that I proved that to you enough times for you just trust me, okay?"

Yami nodded and then held her head back. "I'm sorry. Do you forgive me?" she asked, poking her lips out.

"Hell no," Miego said with a grin, which made her ball up her fist and nail him in the thigh."

"What I tell you 'bout these little ass hands, Yamiah? You gon' make me jack you up. You might have fucked that hoe up, but you can't get with me. I promise you that," he said with a cocky grin before he tightened his arms around her body and pecked her lips.

"Whatever," she said and stood up.

The second she was on her feet, she almost fell back again as a wave of nausea hit and she felt lightheaded.

Miego frowned and looked up at her. "What's wrong?"

"I feel…"

She leaned over the toilet and threw up before she could finish her sentence. Miego jumped up and stepped back, throwing his hands up while he looked down at his body.

"The fuck, shorty? You almost got that shit on me."

Yami lifted her head, rolled her eyes, and wiped her mouth with the back of her hand before she stood and walked to the sink. After she turned the water on, she rinsed her mouth and then grabbed the towel off the rack to wipe her face.

Miego stepped behind her and looked at her through the mirror with a smirk. "Are you pregnant, shorty?"

She frowned and rolled her eyes. "No."

"Then why the fuck you throwing up like that?" he asked.

"I think I ate something that didn't agree with me," she lied. She had already been thinking it, but didn't know for sure. This episode had just confirmed it for her.

"Nah, you're pregnant, shorty. But we're 'bout to find out for sure, let's go," Miego said and unlocked the door.

It wasn't like they were trying or if he even felt like they were ready, but just the idea of it had him happy as hell for some reason. If it was true, then they would figure out the rest. Right now, they were about to take Train home and then hit the first drug store they could get to.

****

"Well?" Miego asked for what was easily the tenth time in the last ten seconds.

Yami ignored him and walked out the bathroom, leaving the three tests she had just taken on the counter. None of the test were ready yet, and she was tired of him asking, so she left him there to find out for himself because if she heard him say 'well' one more time, she was liable to hit him.

"You just gon' ignore me like that, shorty?" Miego asked with a smirk as he followed her. He knew he was aggravating her, but he couldn't help it. He just wanted to know if she was actually pregnant.

"It's been like ten seconds, and I already told you three minutes, so stop saying that," Yami said, sitting down aggressively on the bed.

Miego laughed and stood in front of her. "You just mad cause you know I'm right. So stop tripping."

He reached for her hands and pulled her to her feet.

She looked up at him and frowned. "We don't need a baby, Miego."

"You saying that shit like we're buying a house or a new car or some shit like that. The fuck you mean we don't need a baby?"

"It's too early, and I don't even want to be pregnant right now."

"You can cancel whatever you're thinking 'cause if you are, you're keeping it. That shit ain't even up for debate, shorty." Miego got serious all of a sudden.

"I didn't mean it like that." Yami stepped away from him and he let her. "Do you even want a kid right now? It's not like we planned it."

"You're right, but we both grown as fuck, and knew what could happen every time I didn't use a condom. So don't act surprised, Yamiah. Hell yeah, I want a kid. If you're pregnant then we're having a baby."

She just looked at him conflicted. Ray was still young and they were still new. It wasn't like she didn't trust him to take care of them, but they were still figuring things out, and babies changed everything."

"Look, shorty, can I say that I was sitting around waiting on this shit to happen? No. But it's not like I was running from it either. I'm good either way, and you already know I got you. It's not gon' change anything. I know that's what you're thinking, but it won't. I'm still gon' be me, and you're still gon' be you. You might get fat as hell, but I'm cool with that as long as it's temporary."

Yami wanted to slap the grin off his face, but she couldn't help but laugh. He just didn't care what he said.

"You really make me sick," she said, rolling her eyes.

"Nah, this dick made you sick cause it got your little ass pregnant." He stepped to her and forced her against his chest. "For real though, I'm happy as fuck right now. Just the idea of you carrying my shorty got me smiling and shit. I know we didn't plan it, but so what? Shit happens. You love me, right?"

He looked down and she held her head back just a little and nodded.

"Aight then, that's all that matters. Now let's go see if you carrying my son."

Miego pecked Yami on the lips before the two of them made their way back to the bathroom. He stood in the doorway while Yami leaned over the tests studying them.

"What that shit say, Yamiah?" Miego was getting impatient.

She turned to him, biting into her bottom lip before a grin spread across her face. "Congratulations, Daddy."

It only took a second for his grin to match hers. He stepped in and lifted her off her feet, holding her against his body while her arms circled his neck and her legs circled his waist.

After kissing her intensely, he pulled back and delivered a few pecks. "Why that shit just have me happy as fuck, shorty?"

She shrugged and pecked him again. "Promise me you won't change."

"Yamiah, stop stressing, baby girl. I got you. I got all three of you. You, this baby and Ray. I promise, I got you, shorty."

Again, he kissed her as confirmation and she nodded. Things were definitely the about to change, but she had all the faith in the world in him, so she wasn't worried at all.

Chapter Fifteen

"Miego, please stop, you're getting on my damn nerves." Yami tried to back away from him, but he had a tight grip on her waist as he planted kisses all over her stomach.

She saw it coming when she noticed him sitting at the foot of the bed after she exited the bathroom. Sure enough, the second she was within reach, he pulled her between his legs and focused on her stomach.

"Man, chill. I can spend time with my shorty if I want to." Ignoring her demands, he started kissing her stomach again until she pulled away, but this time he let her.

"Aren't you late anyway?" She tossed over her shoulder before she walked into the closet.

"Why are you clocking my moves, Yamiah?" She could tell from the sound of his voice that he was smiling, so she stuck her head out the closet and shot him a bird.

"I'm not clocking your moves, I just want you to leave so I can have my body to myself for a minute."

After finding a shirt, she pulled it over her head and then rejoined him in the bedroom, where he was standing at the dresser filling his pocket. She tried to move past him, but he took hold of her arm and turned her so that he could pin her against the dresser with his body.

"This body and everything associated with it belongs to me. I'm pretty sure I made that clear this morning when you were begging me for mercy and promising ownership. Don't get that shit twisted." He kept a straight face and waited for her to respond.

"I'm not gonna make it nine months with you acting like this." Yami rolled her eyes then frowned at him.

"Man, let me go before I have to jack your bratty ass up." Miego kissed her on the forehead and then left the room to go check on Ray before he left for his meeting with Train and Memphis.

When Miego walked into the living room, he found Ray sitting on the floor Indian-style in front of the TV. He walked over and lifted her off the floor, tossing her playfully into the air before he brought her down to his chest.

"What you watching, baby girl?"

"Disney Channel," she said, offering up a huge smile before she placed both hands on the side of his face, prompting him to peck her on the lips.

"Where are you going?" Ray asked.

"To meet Uncle Train and Uncle Memphis. Why, you gonna miss me?"

Again, she offered a huge grin before she nodded.

"How about this? You have a good day at school and we can get pizzas and ice cream later."

"Okay," Ray offered through a giggle. She was always on board for ice cream and pizza, which he knew because it was her two favorite things.

"Aight, don't tell your mommy." He pressed his forehead to hers for a second and then lowered her to the floor.

She found her seat again and he took off down the hall to let Yami know that he was leaving. After a goodbye kiss from Yami, she followed him to the door and he waited on the other side until he heard the locks turn. Once he was satisfied that they were good, he was ready to hit the streets.

****

"So, if we do this shit, we keeping any of their people, or we totally rebuilding?" Memphis asked as the three of them sat in Train's vehicle looking across the street at Bank's block boys handling their business.

"If? I thought we already agreed on this shit." Train looked over his shoulder at Memphis.

"You know what I mean. Just answer the fucking question."

"Depends. It didn't mean shit for them to fall in line under Bank, since he used to work for Black, but they might not be feeling that shit once we take over." Miego wasn't looking at either of them because he was still watching the block.

"True, but it is what it is. They can either get on board or fall the fuck off. I don't give a fuck one way or the other," Train said.

"We just gotta make sure we have a good first command in place, 'cause I'm not touching shit and I'm sure neither of you are either." Miego was now focused on them.

"Hell, fuck no. I ain't risking my freedom," Memphis said with a stern look.

"So we need to start making some plans, 'cause as soon as Bank disappears, we gotta be ready to take over. After we check things out and see how they function, then we can get our people up to speed. We call a meeting with their people and let them know what's up. Their foot soldiers lose control of anything except distribution and we ain't telling them shit until we can determine who we keep and who we get rid of," Miego said, thinking out loud.,

"This muthafucker here," Memphis said and chuckled. "You can't shut that shit off, can you?"

"Hell no, he can't, and he was acting like he was gon' walk. What the fuck ever."

"Both of y'all can kiss my ass on some real shit. I'm just trying to make sure we do this shit right and don't end up in a fucking cage, 'cause that ain't the move for any of us. I ain't risking shit that might cost me the opportunity to see my son being born."

"Son? The fuck. Sis pregnant, bruh?" Train spoke up but he and Memphis both had their eyes on him.

"Yeah, man. We found out the day she beat the brakes off Hope." Miego smiled, thinking about Yami going in on Hope.

"The fuck, Miego, that was damn near two weeks ago. Why the fuck you didn't say shit?"

"Yo, take that up with her. She didn't want to tell anybody until we had our official visit. We do that shit tomorrow, so don't say shit or she's gonna kick my ass."

"Your scary whipped ass. I swear you ain't shit no more. Soft as fuck. Scared of Yami's little ass, but congrats. Shit, maybe that will calm your bipolar ass down some." Train grilled him hard for a minute and then laughed.

Miego laughed with him but shot him a bird.

"That's what's up. Shit, maybe now Yaz will stop fucking around and get on board. I'm stepping on thirty. I need to start laying down roots too. Congrats though, fam."

"'Preciate it, but don't say shit to Yaz's annoying ass. You know she can't keep a secret for nothing," Miego said.

"Bruh, you good. I won't say shit 'cause you're right. I bought my sister a car for her birthday. Fucked around and let Yaz help me pick that shit, and Melissa had twenty pictures of it before we even left the lot. I wanted to fuck her up over that shit. She came at me with some, she was gon' find out anyway."

"That shit is on you. I told you not to fuck with her," Miego said with a smirk.

"And I told your ass to stop saying shit about her. You gon' make me fuck you up," Memphis said.

"How you gon' talk shit about her and then get mad at me when I do?"

"Cause you ain't fucking her and I am, so I can do that shit and you can't," Memphis explained with a grin.

"I ought to fuck you up for saying some dumb shit like that. Why the hell you put that image in my head? Yo, I'm out. I can't even fuck with you right now." Miego balled up his face which made Memphis and Train both laugh.

"Yo, hit me later," Memphis said, just before Miego got out.

The three separated and Miego headed home to deprogram his mind after Memphis's statement about Yaz, and then take Ray for pizza and ice cream.

****

Miego looked in his rearview mirror as he made his next turn, and sure enough, the car behind him made the same turn. This had been going on for the last twenty minutes. Originally, he was heading home until he noticed that he was being followed. Not wanting to bring problems to where he laid his head, he kept driving with no real destination.

He peered in his rearview mirror again, trying hard to make out the driver of the car that was following him, but he could only tell that it was a man. The driver kept a safe enough distance to where he couldn't make them out. At this point, he was annoyed and needed to know who was following him, so he pulled into a parking lot, parked, reached under his seat for his gun and chambered it.

Waiting to see what the driver was going to do, his eyes followed the black Benz until it pulled in behind him. The windows were tinted, and from the angle the car was parked, he couldn't see the driver until he stepped out of the vehicle. The guy was tall, solid build, with dreads that hung loosely around his face and shoulder. After the cigar that was in his hand was dropped to the ground, he shut his car door and started towards Miego's car with his hands out to the sides to make it clear that he was unarmed.

Miego got out of his car with his gun in his hand against his leg to make it clear that he was.

"Who the fuck are you, and why the fuck are you following me?"

A smirk spread across his face and his hands moved into the pockets of his dark suit pants. "You can call me Nigel."

"I ain't gon' call you shit, muthafucker, but you need to tell me why the fuck you're following me."

"You're a cocky little muthafucker, aren't you?"

"What I am is no concern of yours, but trust me when I say, you better start giving me a reason not to light your ass up real fucking fast."

Again, the man released a light chuckle. "Look around you. There are people everywhere. You really wanna go back to jail?"

His words annoyed Miego because whoever this was knew things about him, while he didn't have a clue who he was. That wasn't sitting well with him.

"If need be, then fuck yeah, so start talking."

"I know enough about you to know that jail is the last place you wanna be. You can't play daddy from behind bars, now can you? And seems like you're trying to play that role with my granddaughter."

Granddaughter?

The words hit Miego like a ton of bricks. He was face to face with Black's father.

"You obviously got something to say, so get that shit off your chest so I can take my ass home to *MY* family."

Miego watched as Black's father's face grew tight and his jaw clenched. "It's simple. You took something from me, which means that I'm going to take something from you and the bitch who helped you kill my son." His hand was in the air as he pointed at Miego, who now had his gun aimed at him.

Miego's eyes moved around briefly. The streets, along with the restaurant attached to the parking lot that they were in were both full of people. He knew he couldn't pull the trigger, and so did Black's father.

"I might not be able to shoot you here, but trust me, if you come for mine, you lose yours. That's a guarantee, and I've already proven that," Miego said confidently, using every ounce of control he had to keep him from pulling the trigger.

Nigel smiled before he turned to walk away. "I guess that's a chance I'll have to take then."

Miego watched as he got in his car and pulled off. His mind was racing and his first thought was Yami. The second he was in his car, she was the first call he made.

"Shorty, where are you?"

"At the mall with Ray, we're getting her—"

"Go home, right now," Miego demanded.

"Wait, why? What's wrong?"

"Yamiah, just go home. I'll meet you there, and hurry the fuck up," he yelled before hanging up.

His next call was to his mother. He checked on her and she was at the crib with Yanna, so he instructed her to stay in until he talked to her. She didn't like it, but because of his persistence, she agreed.

After that, he checked on Tron, who was out of town helping Jai get set up in her apartment. Since he'd committed to a school in Carolina, she had a place nearby for her and Tajh, who was with his mother. Once he made sure his family was straight, he called Memphis.

"Where you at, fam?"

"At Buffalo Wild Wings with Yaz greedy ass. What's up?"

"Keep her with you."

"What's up, Miego? We got problems?"

"I got one, Black's father just followed me and threatened my family for killing his son. That could mean Yaz too, so keep her with you. I need to figure shit out, but he got a bullet with his name on it. Until I can figure out how to make that happen, keep her with you."

"Nah, we need to figure shit out. Where you heading now?"

"Home, I need to holla at Yami and make sure her and Ray are good. I'll hit you up later, though."

"Aight, bet."

After ending his call with Memphis, he called Train and made plans to put eyes on his mother's building as well as Sylvia's. Yami and her mother might not have the best relationship, but he knew for sure that she'd never forgive herself if anything happened to her. Once he was done making sure everyone was good, he was on his way home to find out what Yami could tell him about Black's father. Nigel would be leaving this earth soon because there was no way he was about to allow him to get to anyone in his family.

Chapter Sixteen

"What took you so long?" Miego yelled the second Yami walked through the door with Ray in her arms.

Ray was knocked out, so Yami ignored him and began moving toward the hallway that led to their bedrooms. He followed, catching up with her after only a few steps, and took Ray from her arms.

Yami opened the door while Miego stepped in and laid Ray across her bed carefully so that he didn't wake her. Once she was situated, he lifted the pink and purple blanket from the foot of her bed and spread it across her tiny body, which was now balled up in the fetal position. When he was done, his hand grasped Yami's pulling her with him. He left the room, closing the door behind the two of them.

The second it closed, she snatched away. "What is your problem?" she asked, narrowing her eyes at him with her voice slightly elevated.

"Come on so we can talk." He took her hand. Again, she snatched away but still followed him to the living room.

"Okay, talk," she snapped from the center of the room once they reached their destination.

"Calm all that shit down. Now is not the time." Miego's hand moved down his face before he folded one across his chest, bending the other at the elbow to pinch the bridge of his nose.

"How the fuck are you gonna yell at me the second I walk through the door, and then tell me to calm dow—"

"Yamiah, shut the fuck up and shit down." Miego pointed at her, now with his voice elevated, but the second his eyes met hers, his mood soften a little. "Please sit down."

After standing her ground for a few moments more, Yami eventually surrendered and walked over to the sofa and sat down. Miego followed, but sat in the leather arm chair next to it, instead of beside her. After he inhaled and let it out slow, he looked right at her but didn't speak.

His behavior was making Yami nervous, so she scooted forward and placed her hand on his knee. "Will you please tell me what's wrong?"

"What do you know about Black's father?"

Confusion set in and Yami looked at him strangely. "Not much, why?"

"You share a kid with him and you don't know shit about his family, Yamiah?"

"No, I don't. Not his father, anyway. He was never really around. Why does that matter?"

"Aren't his parents still married? The fuck you mean he was never around?"

"Just what I said, he was never around. I only spent time with Simone. His father was there a few times, but he didn't really deal with me. To be honest, I don't really think he liked me all that much. Yeah, they're married, but their relationship is strange. It's not like normal married people who seem happy and do stuff together. His dad cheated a lot, Black talked about it all the time, like it was a good thing or something. It was almost like he was proud of it, like he didn't care what it did to his mother. But why do you care?"

"Cause that muthafucker just threatened us. You, me and both of our families, that's why that shit matters." Miego was on his feet pacing, trying to calm himself. Saying it aloud really made it hit home.

"Threatened us, why would he—"

"Because he knows I killed his son, Yamiah. Why the fuck you think?" Miego yelled so loud it made her body jump.

She didn't know what to say. Black and his father were close, but she didn't really think it would come to this, even after Simone mentioned that he took it hard.

"Have you seen him, has he been around?" Miego asked, this time with a little less aggression.

"No."

"Not once?"

"I said no, Miego. But Simone did tell me that he took it hard and that he moved out."

"Fuck. Can this shit get any got damn worse?" Miego punched the wall that he was standing next to, sending his fist right through it.

"You know I have to kill that muthafucker, right? Ain't no way I'm letting him lay a hand on you, your family or mine." Miego eyes were dark and filled with rage as he stared at Yamiah.

She nodded, but didn't speak. Miego watched her for a few moments more before he walked out the room, leaving her standing there. At a loss for words, she stayed put, not knowing what to do. Yamiah took a moment to get her thoughts together before she made her way to their bedroom. She watched him from the doorway, where she found Miego at the foot of the bed, laid back with his folded arms covering his face. Inhaling deep and letting it out slow, she walked over to him, straddled his lap and leaned forward until her head rested on his chest.

"I'm sorry," she released so low, that it was barely audible.

"For what, Yamiah?" Miego's voice was calm, but it vibrated through his chest against the side of her face.

"Being with me complicated your life, and I apologize for that."

Miego removed his arms from his face and sat up, bringing her with him. Once he was upright, they circled his body and he held her firmly against him, kissing her on the forehead."

"Shorty, don't apologize for shit that you can't control. I'm not mad at you and I don't regret anything about my life. Especially not anything that's connected with you. You have to understand that everything about me has changed. You did that shit, Yamiah. I can't even begin to put that into words, but I ain't doing this shit without you or Ray. I'll paint this city red to make sure you're good, so I'm not mad at you. I don't need you apologizing for shit, but hear me when I say, he will die before he touches anybody I love."

"What about you, though? You can't protect all of us and watch your own back. Just like you can't do this without me and Ray, we can't do this without you."

Miego chuckled. "You worried about me, Yamiah?"

She frowned at the fact that he thought it was funny. "Why are you laughing."

"'Cause that shit is funny. I'm good, shorty, you don't have to worry about me."

"You act like you're invincible, Miego, and you're not."

He lifted her chin and connected his lips to hers before looking in her eyes. "You make me invincible. You, Ray, and my little shorty. Can't nobody fuck with me 'cause I got too much to lose, and I promise you that shit ain't happening. Don't worry about me, I'm always gon' be good."

Yamiah couldn't debate that. There was no point in trying because when it came to her safety, Miego had a way of making her believe anything when he really wanted to. For now, she let her arms circle his body, her head rest on his chest, and she closed her eyes. If he said it, it was true, and nothing was going to change that. At least that was what she chose to believe.

****

It was three in the morning and their apartment was dark and quiet. Miego sat in the corner of their bedroom, watching Yami sleep. She looked so peaceful that it calmed him. This was supposed to be a happy time for him. With their doctor's appointment the next day to confirm the addition to their family, he should have been lying next to her resting easy, but that wasn't the case. Instead, he was up, wide awake, one six pack down and working on his second.

His mind was all over the place, trying to figure out how he was supposed to keep his entire family safe. The only resolution was to have them all in one place. After his conversation with Yami, he talked to his mother, giving her minor details about what was going on. The only thing that came from that was a lecture about his lifestyle, which he suffered through long enough to make it clear that things were about to change and she didn't really have a say in the matter.

There was so much she didn't know about his life, but it was necessary in order to keep her mind at ease. She had no idea that he had killed Black and Kia, or that he had been arrested for Kia's murder. Tron and Yanna knew, but he made them both promise to keep it from her, so trying to explain to his mother that she had to move was complicated.

She protested, but after their conversation, Miego had Yami online finding empty apartments in their building. There was a four bedroom available, which he planned to make an offer on first thing in the morning. The goal was to let his mother and sister move into their place, while he and Yami could move to the four bedroom. They needed the space with the baby on the way, so it would work out for everyone.

His mother could complain all she wanted to, but she was moving. Tron was about to graduate in a few weeks and then he would be joining Jai in Carolina, where he had accepted an offer to play at UNC. As of now, all Miego had to do was keep an eye on him until he left. Jai had early graduation and was already there in the apartment that Miego had set up for her and his nephew. Tron had to stay on campus with the team, but Jai and Tajh were in walking distance from campus.

That, he was grateful for. With Tron and his family gone, that was three less people that Miego had to be responsible for. Things were already complicated enough, and he was only one man. Even with their team, Train and Memphis, it was still going to be a struggle to make sure everyone was safe. Miego took things like that personal, which meant that he was going to make it his responsibility to make sure everybody was good. It was necessary, and no matter what, he accepted the responsibility and took it serious at all cost.

Chapter Seventeen

The next morning, Yami woke up to any empty bed. Even as tangled as she was in the sheets, she could still tell that Miego's side of the bed hadn't been touched all night. She had woken up a few times during the night and found him either sitting in the leather chair that was positioned in the corner of their room, or in the living room sitting in the dark.

After a long stretch, she grabbed her phone and checked the time. Realizing that they only had an hour until it was time for her doctor's appointment, she hurried out of bed and went to find him. They hadn't planned to take Ray, so she felt a rush of panic because they would be late if they had to drop her off at daycare like they originally planned.

When she entered the living room, her eyes were drawn to the empty beer bottles that lined the counter before she searched the room and found Miego with his phone to his ear. He was apparently listening to whoever the caller was because he was quiet and nodding, but the second he felt her presence, he held his hand out, signaling for her to join him.

"Yo, Memphis, Yami just got up. Let me hit you back in a few."

"Aight, bet."

Yami reached him and could tell that he had been up all night. His eyes were red and he seemed exhausted. She slid into his lap sideways and kissed his jawline before he leaned in to kiss her lips.

"I was about to come get you. I swear you can't be on time for shit, and we need to go see what's up with my shorty." Miego's hand moved under her shirt, resting flat against her stomach while his thumb moved back and forth across her skin.

"Where's Ray?"

"She left about an hour ago with Memphis and Yaz. They're taking her to his spot until we're done."

Yami didn't bother questioning him about that because she assumed that it had something to do with the situation with Black's father.

She placed her hand on the side of his face. "Did you get any sleep last night?"

"Yeah, for a minute," he lied, not wanting her to worry.

"No, you didn't. You were up every time that I got up."

He smiled and then pecked her lips. "That's your fault, shorty. That baby got you sleeping like a damn bear. I swear you be loud as fuck, growling and shit."

Yami burst out laughing and punched him in the chest. "No I don't, that's not funny."

"Hell, I know it's not funny. I can't get no sleep fucking around with you." He grinned before he grabbed her chin and kissed her lips, which were now poked out.

"You're mean."

He chuckled. "I'm just fucking with you, shorty. Go get dressed though, 'cause we need to get going. I got a bunch of shit to ask this doctor."

"Miego, no. Do not go in there embarrassing me." Her face scrunched up. She couldn't even imagine what on earth might come out of his mouth.

Her animation about his statement made him chuckle before he kissed her neck and lifted her from his lap. "Chill. I ain't gon' embarrass your little ass, Yamiah, but I do have some shit I need to know."

Yami peered at him. "Like what?"

"Go get dressed, you'll see when we get there."

"Oh my God. I can't even with you. This is about to go all kind of wrong," she said, shaking her head.

"Man, I said chill. You better let that shit go before I change my mind and get in there and show my ass. I know you don't want that," Miego said with a grin, which made Yami roll her eyes, turn on her heels, and head toward their bedroom.

She already knew the question was not *if* he was going to embarrass her, but *how much*, he was going to. At this point, it wasn't worth the energy spent worrying about it because she knew that there was no way to control him. He was going to be himself regardless, which was both good and bad. Right now, she was leaning more toward the bad.

"The fuck you sitting over there with your lips poked out for?" Miego asked with a grin after he parked at the doctor's office.

"They're not," Yami said and rolled her eyes. She was pissed because she wanted Starbucks and he refused. Instead, he went to McDonald's drive through and got her orange juice, which was still untouched and sitting in the cup holder.

"You not gon' be feeding my baby all that caffeine, Yamiah. That shit ain't good for you or them."

She sucked her teeth because he was getting on her nerves with all the, 'not good for you and the baby' stuff. She heard it every time she even processed a thought about doing anything. Most of the time she was good with it, but she had to draw the line at her coffee. It was her drug. She was certain that she had a mild addiction to it and couldn't really function without it. He usually wasn't with her in the morning, so he didn't know that she was still drinking it, which worked out perfectly. If she didn't know any better, she would swear that she was currently going through withdrawals because he refused to stop and get it for her.

"It's coffee, Miego, it's harmless."

"Yeah, well until they tell me that, then you ain't drinking that shit, so you can get out your feelings about it." He pointed to the building and then back to her before he leaned across the center console and kissed her on the cheek.

Again, she sucked her teeth before she aggressively pulled the handle to get out.

Miego ignored her tantrum and also got out, after which, he walked around the car to her side. Still not in the mood to deal with him, she was in the process of walking away, but he caught her from behind with a bear hug and rubbed her stomach. "You need to stop acting like a brat, shorty. You can't be a baby and having one at the same time." Miego nuzzled his face in her neck, playfully kissing and biting at her skin until she smiled.

"You really make me sick sometimes."

"Man, how many times I got to tell you that shit? This dick made you sick. Not me, shorty."

"Miego, really?" She tried to shrug him off, but he held on tight and laughed.

"Chill, shorty, I'm just playing with your mean ass. Come on, let's go see about my baby."

"Our baby," Yamiah said sarcastically.

He took her hand in his and chuckled. "If it's a girl, you can get that. But if it's a boy, you can dead that shit. You ain't 'bout to be kissing all over my son, turning him into a little punk. I'm gon' take him under my wing and make him a boss like me."

"I'm not even going to address that," she said, which he found extremely funny.

Having a baby with Miego Grant was about to have her beyond stressed. She could already tell that he was about to make her like difficult.

****

Miego had his head back, his eyes closed, with his arms folded across his chest. His hat was pulled down, covering his eyes while they waited for the doctor. Being up all night was catching up with him, and sitting in their cold, quiet, patient's room, was not helping his situation. He was seconds away from a sleep induced coma, and Yami elected to leave him alone since she knew that he hadn't gotten any sleep last night.

A knock on the door got both of their attention and a tall thin female with long blond hair that was pulled back into a ponytail entered with an exaggerated smile plastered on her face. She grabbed the chart off the back of the door before she shut it and greeted them.

"Well, hello, mom and dad. So, I see this is our first visit. I'm Dr. Sands. Pleased to meet you both."

Yami sat up from the table where she was lying back naked from the waist down, with a sheet covering her and extended her hand.

"I'm Yamiah, and this is Miego. My OB recommended you. I didn't want to do a rotation of doctors and that was all they offer, so she mentioned your practice. She said that you were the best and that you don't do rotations, so here we are," Yami announced.

"Well, I seem to think so, but I'm biased." Sands smiled at Yami before she extended her hand to Miego. "Nice to meet you too, dad."

He nodded and sat up in his chair, before adjusting his hat enough to see her.

"Okay, so let's get started. Says here you had three positive home pregnancy tests and that was..." She paused and read the chart. "A little over two weeks ago. Well congratulations, your tests were correct. You are indeed pregnant." Her smile widened, which made Yami and Miego smile at each other.

"So now that we have that out of the way, we're going to do an ultrasound to see how far along you really are, and get you a due date. How's that sound?"

Not having a clue, Miego looked at Yami, who nodded at Dr. Sands. She walked over to the corner, put her hands on the ultrasound machine and moved it to the side of Yami's table. Once she had it where she wanted it, she moved to the sink, washed her hands, and then pulled on a pair of latex gloves.

Yami said a silent prayer, knowing that Miego was likely about show his ass when he realized what Sands was about to do. She glanced at him and the expression on his face said it all.

Twenty minutes later, they were done. Surprisingly, he had remained quiet and calm, with the exception of the one time he had objected before she got started, to ask questions about if what she was doing would hurt the baby. Other than that, they watched and didn't say much until Sands announced that they were having twins.

At that point, he and Yami both began playing twenty questions with Sands. Even after she printed the ultrasound pictures, they were both still in a mild state of shock, more so Yami than Miego. She remembered how difficult it had been with Ray, and the idea of going through that again times two had her really in her feelings.

"Okay, so now that I've given you the shock of your lives, we're all done here. Do either of you have any questions."

Yamiah, who had been extremely quiet shook her head no, but of course, Miego had a few to get off his chest.

"What about coffee? She drinks that shit like water, and it can't be good for her."

Yami sucked her teeth the second his eyes left Dr. Sands and were on her.

"Coffee is fine, in moderation. No more than a cup a day is recommended, but I'd say every other day."

Yami grinned and stuck her tongue out at him, celebrating her small victory. He mushed her and Dr. Sands laughed. "I assume this had been a topic of discussion," she asked with a grin and they both nodded.

"What about sex? I mean, she good on that, especially with twins and everything?"

"Miego." Yami yelled while her face turned red.

"It's fine. I get that question more than you think. Especially from dads."

Mocking Yami, Miego stuck his tongue out at her and then chuckled while they waited for Sands to answer.

"Sex is fine, and encouraged. It's important to maintain as much normalcy in your relationship as possible because as soon as your little one, or rather little ones, in your case get here, that's going to be extremely difficult and challenging. As mom's tummy begins to grow, you will have to get creative, but as long as there is no discomfort, then I say go for it, have fun with it."

"So what about the babies? I mean, I don't wanna be causing any concussions, brain damage or shit like that," Miego said with the most serious expression, which only lasted for a second because Yami slapped him upside the head, causing a grin to spread across his face.

"I can almost guarantee that will not be an issue," Dr. Sands said.

"I don't know, Doc, I ain't fucking with no minor league," Miego said and then leaned back so that Yami couldn't reach him.

"Oh my God. Please forgive him. It's think he's the one with brain damage," Yami said, narrowing her eyes at him.

"He's fine. Perfectly normal questions, and Miego, I assure you that no matter how endowed you are, you will not be at risk of giving your babies concussions or brain damage. Just do what feels natural, follow mom's lead about what feels good, and you guys should be fine."

"No hell, I already know what feels good, so I don't need to follow shit," he said, laughing at himself.

"Well, seems to me that you guys have it all figured out, or at least you do, dad," Dr. Sands said with a slight chuckle. "If you have any other questions, any at all, please feel free to call my service. Congratulations, and I'll see you two in a month."

"'Preciate it." Miego accepted the hand that Dr. Sands extended to him and then she did the same to Yami before she left the two of them alone.

The second the door closed, Yam threw the sheet back and swung her legs over the side of the table. "I can't believe you. I swear, you just do too much."

He found her reaction funny. "The fuck you mad for? She asked if I had any questions. I bet she hears that shit all the time, Yamiah. Hell, she thought that shit was funny."

"So what if she hears it all the time? I really didn't need you asking it," Yami said, trying to stay mad as she stepped into her panties and then her jeans. But the second she looked at him, his smile forced one on her face and she laughed.

"Don't trip, you know that you wanted to know that shit too. Don't even front."

"I already knew that, asshole. I'm just surprised that you didn't flip out when she did the ultrasound," Yami said, pointing to the machine. She just expected him to really embarrass her when that happened.

"Nah, I knew about that shit. Tron told me after he had to go through it wit' Jai. Fucked him up watching them do it, so I was ready for that. Besides, that little shit ain't fucking with me, so I wasn't worried." Miego pointed to the wand Sands used to do the vaginal ultrasound and then winked at Yami.

"Wow, really?" Yami lifted her purse and stood by the door so that they could leave, but Miego threw his arm around her.

"You ready for this, shorty? We're about to have twins, Yamiah. That shit is crazy as fuck."

"No, I'm not, but you better not leave me. I can't do this by myself."

"Yamiah, chill. The fuck I'm gon' leave you for? Well, I might after you have them 'cause I know your ass is gon' blow up, especially with twins. So, I mean, if you can't drop that weight, we gon' have some issues. We can talk about it first and do some Weight Watchers or some shit like that, but if you can't work that out, we gon' have to do some co-parenting."

"You are such an asshole, I swear."

Miego burst out laughing and then kissed her. "Chill, you know I'm just fucking with you, shorty. I'll love you no matter what. We in this shit."

"You better."

"You better stop doubting that shit. Now let's go so we can tell everybody. It was hard as hell trying to keep this shit a secret."

Yami rolled her eyes. "Secret?" So you didn't tell Train and Memphis?"

"Nah, why?" Miego smiled and gave her the side eye.

"'Cause I know you're lying, but I'll find out soon enough." Yami pulled the door open and the two headed to the front desk to get scheduled for her next appointment.

She didn't know for sure if he told, but she had a feeling that he did. Train and Memphis were like his brothers, so it was likely that they already knew. Either way, she knew she could make them confess, but right now her mind was stuck on the fact that not only was she pregnant, but with twins. Things were definitely about to change. Whether that was good or bad, she didn't know yet, but there was no going back now.

Chapter Eighteen

"You know I'm thirty-eight hot with you right now? I really wanna slap your yellow ass," Yaz said, pointing to her sister. Right after the words flew out of her mouth, she looked across the room at her niece to make sure she wasn't looking.

"Why, though? I needed to make sure, before we told anybody. You were the first to know. We came straight here after we found out, just so that I could tell you." Yami looked at her sister with a childlike grin before she snuggled closer to her on the sofa.

"Hoe, please. You only came here because you had to get Ray. Don't play me, Yamiah, and you should have told me. I would have gone with you this morning."

"That's exactly why I didn't tell you," Yami said with a frown.

"Whatever, man." Yaz sucked her teeth and then placed her hand over her sister's stomach. "Twins, huh? They're about to have you stressed out, and you better pray they don't come out like his ignorant ass."

"You need to chill with that." Yami laughed as the thought of two mini Miego's flashed through her mind.

"Don't act like you not already thinking it. Are you going to tell Mom?"

"Nope."

"Like not at all, or just not now?"

Yaz was surprised by her sister's answer. Yami was always the one to make excuses for their mother, but after the way she acted at Ray's party, Yamiah hadn't been to see her, called her, or even mentioned her name.

"For now, not at all. Why would I set myself up like that, Yazmine? You already know she's not going to have anything good to say about it, and I'm not going there with her. I'm happy and I want to stay that way."

"I guess I understand that. Maybe she'll get her act together because it don't make no sense to be so hateful."

"Honestly, I'm over it. I'm good, Ray's good, and if she can't respect that then I can't respect her. Blood doesn't give you a pass."

"True."

"Yo, we need to go make a run real quick." Miego fell into the sofa next to Yami, causing her body to lean into his because of their weight difference.

"I thought we were going to tell your mom and sister about the babies," Yami said, dipping her body under Miego's arm so that she was cradled against his side. Once she was situated, his hand moved under her shirt onto her stomach.

"We are, in a little while though. Me and Memphis gotta go handle something real quick first. Just stay here until I get back." He leaned down and kissed the side of her neck. "And don't be feeding my babies no bullshit while I'm gone either." He playfully narrowed his eyes at her, just to annoy her even more.

"You know what, if you keep this up. We're not going make it for the next thirty-two weeks."

"The fuck you mean thirty-two weeks, shorty? Doc said you were eight weeks. I might not have graduated high school and shit, but I ain't dumb and your math ain't adding up. You don't carry that damn baby for ten months."

Yaz and Yami both looked at each other and laughed. Just as Memphis joined them, sitting on the arm of the sofa near Yaz.

"What's so funny?"

"Shit, I'm trying to figure that out myself."

"Pregnancy last forty weeks, so I have thirty two weeks left."

"That's longer than nine months, shorty."

"Kinda... not really... it's complicated."

"She low key trying to say your simple ass can't understand, bruh," Memphis said and laughed.

"That is not what I'm saying." Yami glared at Memphis and then placed her hand on Miego's chest before looking up at him.

"You shitting me, that's what the fuck it sounds like, Yamiah." He knocked her hand away and Yaz laughed.

"I'm just saying, you act so damn ignorant all the time, maybe she's just don't want to embarrass you with a complicated explanation." Yaz smirked at Miego.

"Mind your business, Yazmine." Memphis lowered his arm around her and pulled her against the side of his leg, but Miego reached around Yami and mushed Yaz in the head so hard that she felt her neck pop.

"You play too much, stupid ass. You just made my neck pop."

Miego smirked back at her. "So, that's what the fuck you get. All up in this shit over here," he said with a smug grin.

Yaz looked up at Memphis, who grinned and kissed her on the forehead. "Don't look at me, I told you to mind your business, shorty."

"Really, Memphis?" Yaz yelled.

"You're wrong for that." Yami said, but she laughed because it was funny.

Miego just shrugged and kept it moving. "Yo, you ready?" He glanced at Memphis before pulling Yami to her feet with him as he stood. He kissed her and then walked over to Ray and yanked her off the floor.

"Be good, baby girl, and don't let your mommy eat any junk. It's not good for the babies."

"I won't."

He planted kisses all over her face while she giggled and tried to shield herself. When he was done, he lowered her to the spot she was in on the floor, where she was watching a movie on her iPad.

Miego and Yami didn't know what type of reaction they were going to get from Ray about the fact that her mother was pregnant, so when her only response was to ask if she could talk to them, they were thrilled. Yami nodded and Ray had pressed her face to her mother's stomach and whispered something that neither of them could hear, and she refused to tell them what she said. Miego planned to bribe her later with candy, but he didn't press her.

Ray didn't seem concerned in the least bit about the additions to their family. In fact, she wanted to go to the store to buy stuff for them, but Yami explained that they were going to wait for a while until they knew if the babies where going to be girls, boys or both. After that, Ray was done and went right back to playing like nothing had changed.

"Aight, shorty, we'll be back. Take care of my babies."

He delivered a few more kisses. Memphis and Yaz made up and did the same. Yami and Yaz walked their men to the door and locked up after they left. The two of them got comfy to watch TV while they discussed the babies and how exited they both were about the new additions to the family.

****

"So, with everything going, I assume we waiting on this shit with Bank." Train sat across from Miego as they separated the product that they were about to distribute.

Memphis had paid in on the shipment that they had just received, so now the three of them were now equal partners. He had been having issues with his suppliers with the guns he was selling, so for now, he was putting that on hold.

"The fuck we need to wait for? I'm not 'bout to put my life on hold for him. Ain't shit changing but the fact that we 'bout to keep eyes on everybody to make sure they're good. Other than that, he can kiss my ass. You should know me better than to ask some dumb shit like that," Miego said.

"Yo, I was just asking, bruh. You got twins on the way and shit, and got that muthafucker's father coming for you. But if you cool, then I'm cool." Train held a closed fist up to Miego, which he met with his.

"So how the fuck he know, anyway?" Memphis asked after he zipped the duffle bag he had just loaded and set it on the floor next to him.

"The fuck if I know, and I don't really care, but I confirmed it when he started making threats. What I do know is if he touches anyone I care about I'm gon' paint this got damn city red."

They all looked at each other and silently agreed. There wasn't anything else to say about that.

"What about your moms, yo. Did you get her a place in your building?"

"Sort of. I'm moving her and Yanna into ours, and then me and Yami moving up two floors into a four bedroom. I called and handled it first thing this morning."

"What'd she say?"

"Who?"

"Your mom. Ms. Ginette been in the same spot since as long as I can remember. She cool with leaving?"

Miego chuckled. "She don't know yet. I mentioned it last night and told her some shit was about to change, but I didn't tell he what yet."

"The fuck you mean she don't know?"

"I mean, I told her I was doing it and she told me she wasn't moving, but she don't know I actually bought a new place."

"So how the fuck you gon' make that happen, bruh?" Train looked at Miego like he had lost his mind. He knew Ginette well. Very well, in fact, which meant that if she didn't want to move, she wasn't moving.

"Bruh, she don't have a choice. I'll burn that bitch down so she can't go back if I have to. She might as well get that shit out her head. She's moving."

"You're tripping. She gon' fuck your ass up for telling her what she's gon' do."

"Damn, she go hard like that?" Memphis asked. He had met her at Ray's party, and as far as he could tell, she was quiet and sweet.

"Muthafucker, what? You have no idea. You think Yami got him by the balls? Ms. Ginette don't play. She'll have his ass in tears."

Memphis laughed and then pointed at Miego. "You bold as fuck trying to make your moms move without her permission. I mean, I get why, but damn, bruh. Let me know when it's going down so I can be there to watch." Memphis smirked.

"The fuck outta here with that. Ain't go be shit to watch but her packing her damn clothes."

"Yeah aight, we'll see 'bout that." Train laughed. "But speaking of that shit, we just sitting on this right now, or we going after this muthafucker?"

"I don't know shit about him yet, so for now we're just chilling. We'll keep an eye on everybody, being cautious too and shit. But like I said, I ain't running scared, fuck him. If he wanna come at me again, let him. He can catch one just like his son. Hell, he would have if his bitch ass wouldn't have fronted me in broad daylight on a street full of people. Either way, I don't give fuck. We got life to live and money to be made, so for now, that's our focus."

Memphis looked at Miego and shook his head. "This muthafucker here, with his gangster ass," he said and then chuckled.

"Fuck yeah. A boss gon' be a boss, and I'm riding that shit until I'm six feet under. Now fuck with it," Miego said, making Train laugh because he knew how serious he was.

The three of them finished splitting up the product to prepare for their deliveries. In the next few days, they had two guys coming up from each state they supplied to deliver money and pick up their product. Until then, they would keep it stashed at their warehouse.

Neither of them kept their hands on product or money for long, other than the safes of cash they kept at their homes. They kept minimal contact with everything, since they were supplying now and not in sales, and that was just the way they liked it. They had a steady flow of money coming in, with very little headache.

Aside from a trip every month to check on their locations, they really didn't have to do shit. That was the beauty of being smart enough to have good people in place. As far as business was concerned, Miego and Train could be considered magna cum laude of the drug game. Now that Memphis was on board, they were a triple threat, and nothing could touch them.

Chapter Nineteen

"You know you're pretty as fuck right now," Miego said as he walked into the bathroom and leaned against the door frame.

Yami was standing in front of the mirror wearing a pink sundress that was printed like a bandana. It was secured around her neck, exposing most of her back, but hung loosely around her body, stopping just below her knees.

"I should always be pretty to you, not just right now," she said with a smirk, looking at him through the mirror while she secured her hair in a low ponytail.

Summer was here, and she was grateful to have a break from school for a minute. With Ray going to daycare most days, she and Miego spent a lot of time together when he wasn't with Train or Memphis, and she was loving it. Well, with the exception of him hovering and obsessing over everything she did because of the babies.

"You are, but we're talking about right now, and right now, I feel like bending you over that counter." He entered the bathroom while Yami turned to face him. It only took him a minute to press his body against hers and for his hands to make it under her dress, but she grabbed both of them, trying to stop him.

"Would you quit it? Your mom and sister will be here any minute, so this is not happening."

"So you're telling me no?" A grin spread across his face, which had Yami struggling to keep her expression neutral, so she bit into her bottom lip and nodded.

"When she did, he gently grabbed her chin and kissed her, while using the other hand to explore her body again.

"Didn't I just say no?"

"Nah, you didn't. You nodded yes." His hands were already moving her panties down her thighs.

"I nodded yes because you asked me if I was telling you no."

Yami kept her eyes on his and moaned a little when she felt his fingers move across her clit and then enter her. Her head went back and her eyes closed while he let them glide in and out of her center, which was already warm and wet.

"May bad, shorty, I misunderstood. You want me to stop though?" he asked, shoving his fingers as deep as they would go while his thumb applied pressure to her clit and he kissed her neck. "Yamiah, you want me to stop, shorty?" he asked again, removing his fingers just enough to caress her lower lips and then shoving them in her again.

Instead of answering, her hands moved to the sweatpants that he was wearing and slid inside them enough to release his hardening member. Her hands moved up and down his shaft causing it to harden and grow a few more inches before she looked down at it with a grin.

That was confirmation enough because Miego firmly grabbed her waist and then lifted her onto the counter. It reminded her of the last time they had a session like this, which was at her sister's house after the Hope situation. Thoughts of how rough he was caused her center to pulse a little more. She gripped the counter and waited while he grabbed himself and let the head tap her clit before moving across her lower lips, just to tease her.

"Stop playing, Miego, and you better hurry up," Yami whined.

He had started something, and she was ready to finish it. Pregnancy had made her extremely horny all the time, but it wasn't a problem because Miego was all too eager to satisfy anytime she was in need of a fix.

With a light chuckle, he pressed his lips against hers. "Why you rushing? Didn't you just tell me no?"

Yami refused to answer, and instead grabbed his waist with one hand, and his erection with the other and pulled him near her. Again, he laughed, but gave in. With one deep stroke, he pushed inside her and had to brace himself.

"Fuck, shorty. You gon' make me bust fast as hell. This shit don't make no sense."

He closed his eyes and started slow steady strokes, trying hard to control what he was feeling. His hands firmly gripped her ass while pulling her hips so close to the edge that his body in front of her was the only thing keeping her from hitting the floor.

"Miego, don't let me fall," Yami whispered through labored breaths, letting her hands fall back behind her while Miego continuously drilled into her body.

"Shut up, little girl, I'm not gon' let your ass fall."

To make sure he didn't, he took a step closer to the counter, which sent him so deep inside her that she yelled out. "Don't be so rough, Miego. You know that shit hurts."

"You should be used to it by now, shorty," he said with a smirk, digging deep again.

Yami bit her lip in an effort to keep quiet, which only made him go harder since he knew what she was doing. That made her try to scoot back away from him, but he gripped her waist hard and pulled her back.

"Stop moving, damn," Miego snapped, hitting her deep again a few more times until they heard the doorbell sound.

"Fuck," he grunted but kept going.

"That's probably your mom and sister."

"Then you better hurry up and cum, shorty, or they're gon' be out there until you do. I ain't stopping until you cum, Yamiah."

Knowing that they were pressed for time, his thumb moved to her clit. He applied pressure and began to massage it while he focused on his strokes. Miego could feel his nut rising, but he wouldn't let it go until she got hers, so he kept working until he felt her body tremble. Once he knew she was ready to release her orgasm, he pumped harder and faster until he exploded inside her and his body tensed up.

Yami frowned and slapped his arm. "That shit hurt, Miego."

"Man, chill. You're good, and you like it anyway, so I don't know what the fuck you complaining for." He grabbed her waist and helped her off the counter before yanking a washcloth off the brushed nickel bar that was on the wall above the sink

"Don't use that," Yami said and snatched it from him.

"Why the fuck not?"

"It's for decoration," she said and attempted to put it back, but he snatched it out her hand and ran it under the water that he had just turned on before she could stop him.

"Why did you do that?"

"Cause this ain't our spot anymore. My moms gon change that shit anyway, so stop tripping." He cleaned himself up and then handed the towel to Yami before he pecked her lips and left the bathroom.

She rolled her eyes and mumbled, "Asshole."

He heard her and laughed. "I'm your asshole, though, and you love me, so I'll be that. Hurry up, shorty. I'm 'bout to go open this door."

Yami cleaned herself up and then sprayed down the counter with bathroom cleaner. Once she had everything like she wanted, she sprayed air freshener and then shut the door. She prayed that they wouldn't know what had just gone on before they arrived. Even though they were grown, stuff like that was still awkward for her, and the last thing she wanted was for his mother to question her about sex with her son.

****

"Ma, how long you gon' be mad at me?" Miego walked up behind his mother and let his arms wrap around her body.

She was in the kitchen of what used to be his and Yami's apartment, but now belonged to her and his sister. It took two weeks after the purchase to get their new place ready, but the second he got the okay, he had Yami ordering furniture for their new place since they were leaving what they had for his mother and sister. The only thing they were changing was Ray's play room, which used to be Yami's old room.

All of Ray's toys were sent two floors up to their new place, and Miego let his sister order a new bedroom set. They left Ray's room like it was, since they were now in the same building, and Ginette insisted on having space for her, since she planned on Ray being there a lot.

"I'm not mad at you. I just don't like being told what to do. I'm the parent, Miego, not you."

Miego planted several kisses on her cheek before he let he go, and then leaned on the counter in front of her.

"I know that, but I'm the only man in your life, and I want to take care of you. So stop complaining and just be happy."

"How can I be happy when the only reason you're forcing me to be here is because you got yourself into something that is putting all of us in danger?"

"Ma, chill with that. You ain't in danger, not like that. Shit, you were in more danger living around those people at your old spot."

"Don't cuss me, Miego James Grant. You might be grown, but you're not that damn grown." She pointed her finger at him, which made him laugh.

"My bad, ma, but can you just be happy for me, please?" He offered up sad pouty eyes, trying to win her over, which made her suck her teeth and go back to washing the pans that she insisted on bringing from her apartment.

"You want me to be happy about the fact that someone is trying to hurt my son and my grandchildren. I can't do that," she said.

Miego hated that he even told her the little bit of information he gave her. She only knew that he had enemies who could try to hurt him by getting to her. She didn't know that it was Black's father, and she wouldn't if he had any say in it.

"Well, either way, I'm glad you're here. I like having you close."

"Mmmhmm," was all she said until Ray came running into the kitchen and hugged her legs.

"I'm glad you're here too, Nana GiGi. I can see you all the time."

That was enough to change her whole attitude. She still wasn't thrilled about the reason behind it, but anything that kept her close to Ray and the babies that were on the way was enough to make her smile

"I'm glad I'm here too, pretty girl."

"Can we watch a movie?" Ray asked, bouncing in place.

"We sure can. Just let me finish up in here. You go pick," Ginette said after leaning down to kiss Ray on the forehead.

Ray took off running and Miego stood there grinning at his mother until she couldn't take it anymore.

"What, child?"

"You're welcome."

He stole another kiss on her cheek and then went to go find his sister and Yami.

Chapter Twenty

"Let's do this shit." Miego chambered the first round in his gun then nodded at Train and Memphis before he climbed out of Train's vehicle.

The three of them had been waiting outside of Bank's apartment for him to come home. Bank was so wrapped up in the female he was attempting to kick game to on the phone, that he didn't even realize that they were on him until he felt Miego's gun pressed to the back of his head. It was dark, and the lighting outside of his building was shitty.

"Tell her you'll call her back, bruh. If you get to live, that is." Miego smirked, feeling a rush

Bank held one hand up while he removed his phone for his ear and ended the call.

"The fuck is this shit?" he snarled as soon as Memphis stepped in front of him with his gun aimed at his forehead.

"This, muthafucker, is a negotiation. You're about to negotiate with us whether you live or die. How's that sound?" Memphis said with a smirk.

"I ain't negotiating shit. You wanna kill me then do it."

"This muthafucker," Memphis said.

"Bruh, you say that shit a lot. What, is that your catchphrase or some shit like that?" Miego said and laughed before stepping in front of Bank so that he was side by side with Memphis."

"Shit, do I? I don't even be paying attention," Memphis said.

"Yeah, you do. All the got damn time," Train added.

"So fucking what?" Memphis said and chuckled. "But back to this muthafucker, though. So you cocky, huh? You really don't give a fuck, do you?" Memphis asked.

"Nah, I don't. Now what?"

Miego held his gun up and fired a shot the was so close to Bank's head that it grazed his ear. He ducked and grabbed his head.

"You a got damn lie. Your ass ain't ready to die, or you wouldn't have flinched, so let's take a ride." Miego looked Bank right in the eyes with a smug grin on his face.

"Hell no, you wanna talk, do that shit right here."

"Nah, you ride or you die now," Train said, cocking his gun.

"Where the fuck you taking me?"

"Don't worry about that, let's go."

Memphis grabbed his arm and checked him for weapons. After finding only one in his waistband, he handed it to Miego, and then tugged Bank enough to turn his body in the direction he wanted him to go. Miego shoved Bank in the back to make him start walking.

They headed to Train's ride. He got in the driver's seat while Memphis and Miego both got in the back, with Bank in the center. Over the past month they had been watching Bank's operation, and knew just about all his people and how they functioned. Train drove them to the abandoned house that Bank used for meetings as well as to store product and money.

"The fuck we doing here?" Bank asked, looking around.

"Just get out the fucking truck. You asking too many questions and annoying the fuck outta me," Miego said.

"Shit, I got the right. You holding guns on me talking about I'm gon' have to negotiate for my life."

"This muthafucker," Memphis said and then laughed. "You right, I do say that shit a lot."

"Told your dumb ass," Miego said.

Once they were inside, they made Bank sit in a chair while they laid out their plans.

"Here's what's going down. You're 'bout to call your people and tell them you're having an emergency meeting. If everybody shows up, you live. If they don't, well you already know how negotiations work," Miego said with a grin.

"And why the fuck would I be stupid enough to do that?"

"That ain't stupid, what would be stupid is you not doing it, so that's on you, bruh," Memphis smirked.

"How do I know you won't kill me anyway? I mean, shit, you killed Black," Bank said with a scowl on his face.

"I killed Black? That's news to me? I guess I be killing muthafuckers in my sleep or some shit like that, 'cause I don't recall taking his life."

"What the fuck ever. Just keep it one hundred. I assume this is about you taking over my shit."

"Your shit? Damn, Black can't get no credit for that? I mean, he did start that shit," Train said.

"It's my shit. All he did was run his mouth and cause problems. I don't handle business like that. I works for mine."

"Oh yeah?" Train asked.

"Hell yeah, while he was running round fucking women, I was making money."

"So you mad cause you weren't getting no ass? That's fucked up, bruh. You gotta make time for both. Everybody needs balance in their life." Miego wore a smug grin.

"Fuck you. I get pussy, muthafucker. I just make sure I'm getting bread too."

"Stop fucking with his ass, Miego," Memphis said.

"Aight, aight, seriously though. You doing your thing, so here's the deal. You call your people, get them here, let them know they no longer work for you, that they work for us—"

"Hell no, I'm not doing that shit." Bank cut Miego off before he could finish.

"Aight then, you can die right now. Either way, we taking your shit," Train said, pressing his gun into Bank's forehead.

"Hold up, wait. So if I do that, then what? You let me live and I work for you?"

"Yep, that simple. We'll have our people in place to make sure you ain't on no fuck shit, but other than that, you live and you get to keep making money. Only difference is we own it and we determine how much you make. You good with that?"

"Do I have a choice?" Bank snapped.

"My man. Finally seeing the light." Memphis held his hand up to dap Bank, but Bank glared at him and didn't move.

"Well, damn, muthafucker. How we gon' be a team but you can't show love? That's fucked up, yo." Memphis laughed and stepped back.

"Start calling," Miego said.

Bank leaned back and pulled his phone out. He was beyond pissed. His territory made a lot of money, but he knew that they weren't going to pay him near what he was bringing in, and he was fuming about the idea of having to work for them. But as of now, he didn't have a choice. It was agree or die, and he damn sure wasn't about to die. That didn't, however, stop him from mentally planning how he was going to handle the three of them and take his territory back. If they thought they were about to just take his shit and he was going to stand back and let them do it, then they were seriously fucked in the head, as far as he was concerned.

****

"Sup shorty, you good?" Miego said as he eyed the room full of men.

There were roughly twenty plus present, and after checking them for weapons, they were all standing around waiting to find out why they were there. Bank was standing in the front while Train had his gun to his temple. They only paused their meeting so that Miego could answer Yami's call. With Black's father making threats and her being pregnant, he refused to not take her calls.

"I'm fine. It's late, when are you coming home?"

"It won't be long, but check it, shorty. I'm in the middle of something important, so if you're good, I need to call you back."

"Will you bring me a milkshake?"

"Hell no, so you can be blowing up the damn room all night with gas and shit."

"Miego, please. I really want one."

"Fine, but I got to go, and if you start that shit, you're sleeping in there with Ray. I mean it too." He laughed.

"Love you, hurry up," she said, satisfied that she was getting her way.

"Love you too, with yo bratty ass."

Miego slid his phone into his pocket and removed his gun from the waistband of his jeans before he joined Train and Memphis again.

"Aight, so I guess you're wondering why the fuck you're here, and why he got a gun pressed to his head, right?"

They all looked at Miego but didn't say a word.

"Damn, they don't like your ass, yo," Memphis said with a chuckle, causing Miego to mug him.

"Aight, let's get this shit over with. You have a new boss, well three to be exact." Miego nodded at Train and Memphis behind him. "You got a problem with that, then walk now. You wanna keep making money, then stay."

They all looked at each other. A few of them mumbled stuff, but no one moved.

"So you taking his shit?" one cat asked, stepping to the front.

"Yeah, you got a problem with that?" Train asked.

"Nah, money is money, and you promise we gon' keep making it, then I'm good. I know who y'all are, and I know you 'bout business. Fuck all that other shit. You good to me, I'm good to you."

"That's fucked up, Hoss. Where's your damn loyalty?" Tech said, pointing at him.

It was bad enough that he had to work for Bank after Black died, but now them. He was annoyed because he had been working hard to gain position with Bank. Working under the three of them meant that he was always gonna be just a worker.

"My loyalty is to green. If they gon keep my pockets fat, I'm down."

"So you got a problem with that?" Miego asked, aiming his gun at the Tech.

He knew exactly who he was, and knew that he was an ass kisser. They hadn't planned to keep him around for long, and damn sure weren't about to let him handle anything.

"Nah, I'm cool. I guess he's right." He shrugged.

"Anybody else got issues?" Miego asked.

A bunch of heads shook to say no, and eyes roamed the room. "I guess it's settled. You got a new boss then." Miego turned to Bank and smiled.

The fire in Bank's eyes was laughable to Miego because Bank had no idea that he was about to die. They got what they needed from him, and there was no way they would let him stay on their team. You couldn't buck on a man like that and not expect him to feel some type of way about it. Bank would cross them the first chance he got, or even worse, try to kill them.

"That's it, then," Memphis said.

"Make smart choices and you don't have anything to worry about, but if you think you gon' cross us, you will die. Get back to business as usual, and we'll meet up soon to lay shit out. When you get back, you'll notice our people on the block. They're in charge. You got issues, go to them first, and then they'll come to us. Other than that, let's make some money," Miego said, dismissing them.

The men started heading out the building. A few approached to say a few words or shake hands with them, but other than that, things went smoothly.

Once everyone was gone, Bank looked at the three of them, waiting to see what was next. He was mad as hell and ready to get the fuck out of there.

"You got what you wanted. What now?" Bank snarled.

Miego chuckled, lifted his gun and shot him right in the head.

His body hit the floor and then Miego lowered his gun.

"Damn, your ass couldn't give no warning? The fuck, look at my damn shirt," Train said, pointing to the blood on his body.

"My bad, bruh. You know I got you," Miego said with a smirk.

"I swear, I hate your ass," Train said, checking out his shirt again.

"Yo, you think he knew he was gon' die, or you think he really thought we were going keep him on?"

"That muthafucker thought he was going be first in command, all while he was plotting to kill our black asses." Miego chuckled.

"You're right," Train agreed.

"Aight, let's get this body handled so that we can get the fuck outta here."

The three of them rolled the body up in plastic. Double bagged it in oversized trash bags using duct tape to seal them, and then carried the body to the old van they had purchased for the job. Once they were done, they drove it across town and dumped it at a landfill. Miego wiped the gun clean that he used to kill Bank, disassembled it, and left pieces of it all over the city as they drove across town to get rid of the body.

Once they were done, everyone went their separate ways. He stopped to get Yami the milkshake that she requested and then headed home. He was ready to shower, climb in bed, and wrap his arms around her. They had just made a major move, and between that and knowing that Black's father was still out there, he just needed a minute to let everything go. She was his escape from reality, and when her body was close to his, nothing else seemed important. He need that right now, even if it was temporary.

Chapter Twenty-One

"Yamiah, this is Doctor Sands, I just wanted to let you now that I sent all of your paperwork over to Mercy. I know you were anxious about getting registered for your tour, so they should have you in the system. You can stop by anytime to fill out the paperwork. Once they have you registered, you can tour the maternity floor and get signed up for your Lamaze classes. Give me a call if you have any questions."

Yami disconnected her call and looked back at Ray. They were on their way to meet Miego's mom to do some shopping, but since she got the call from Dr. Sands, she decided to take a detour and go ahead and get registered. She was already over the whole process and wanted to get everything in order. Since she had been through it before with Ray, and Miego hadn't. She felt like it as only fair for him to have the full experience. That included the two-hour session and tour that the hospital offered for new parents.

"Hey, baby girl. Can we make one stop before we go meet Nana GiGi?"

"No, I want to go now."

"But it will be really quick. Mommy just has to go to the hospital to sign some papers. Can I do that please, and then we can stop and get milkshakes before we go meet Nana GiGi.

Sold! Ray's face lit up. She was on board for anything that included some type of ice cream.

"Yami started her car and pulled away from the building, en route to the hospital.

"Mommy, will I have to share my room with the babies when they get here?"

"If they're girls, maybe, but if they're boys, then no. Do you want to?"

"If I have a sister, she can share with me, but not a brother." Ray balled up her little face.

"Why did you look like that, Ray?" Yami asked watching her daughter's face in the rearview mirror.

"Because I don't like boys."

I'm sure Miego will be thrilled to hear that.

"But you like Tajh, you play with him all the time."

Ray frowned. "But only a little bit."

"But if it's your brother, you'll like him a lot. Just wait, you'll see."

"Can Miego be my dad too? I was here first, and he loves me too."

Ray's question threw Yami a little, but it made her smile. Ray wasn't thrilled about the idea of sharing Miego, especially after she kept hearing everyone referring to the twins as his babies, and that he was their father. No one ever referenced him that way when it came to Ray, even though he was, in every sense of the word. Either way, she was smart and had noticed that.

"Do you want that? Do you want Miego to be your dad too?"

"I miss my daddy, but Miego can be my daddy too. He loves me and he's here."

Yami had a rush of emotions flood her all at once. She had been doing that a lot since she found out she was pregnant, but it was far worse than it was when she was pregnant with Ray. She didn't know if it was the twins causing a double dose of hormones, or if it was Ray's words that hit her hard. Whatever the case, she felt tears sliding down her face.

She quickly used the back of her hand to wipe them away before Ray could see her.

"If that's what you want, I'm sure he won't mind at all," Yami said.

"Okay," was all Ray said before she leaned over and lifted her iPad from the seat and focused on it.

Yami drove the rest of the way to the hospital, stuck in her feelings. For the first time in a long time, everything was starting to fall in line, and she felt grateful for every second of happiness she was experiencing.

After Yami pulled into the parking deck and parked, her phone went off. Her Bluetooth picked up and Miego's voice filled the car.

"Where are you and baby girl, shorty?"

"At the hospital," Ray yelled from the backseat, causing Yami to frown, knowing that Miego was about to skip right to the worst possible scenario in his mind.

"What's wrong, shorty? Why you at the hospital?" Miego asked, sounding panicked.

"Calm down, I'm just here to get registered for the hospital tour. Dr. Sands left me a message and said that she sent my paperwork over, and since I was already out, I decided to go ahead and get it done now."

"Man, you need to tell me shit like that, shorty. I was nervous as hell."

"I just found out. Sorry."

"Miego, guess what?"

"What's that, baby girl?"

"I get a milkshake, and Mommy said that if I want, you can be my daddy too. Not just the babies."

He chuckled at how she added something so important in the same sentence with getting a milkshake, like it just made perfect sense to her.

"Word, is that what you want, baby girl?"

"Yes, silly," Ray said and grinned.

"That's what's up. So does that mean I get a milkshake too?"

"Nope, you're not here," Ray said, "But I'll tell Mommy to bring you one. Mommy, can we bring him one?"

"Nah, you're good, baby girl. I'll see you at home after you help Nana go shopping, okay."

"Okay, will you bring me a surprise?"

Again, he laughed. "Yeah, I got you."

"Do I get a surprise too?" Yami asked.

"Man, gone with that."

"I'm serious," Yami said with a slight pout.

"Yeah, aight, I got you, but just remember you asked for it, when you get it."

Knowing exactly what he meant, Yami sucked her teeth and then glanced at Ray.

"I'm not playing with you."

Miego burst out laughing. "Don't be like that, shorty."

"Whatever, man. Let me go so I can get this over with."

"Aight, text me when you're heading home, and I'll meet you there. I love you."

"Love you too."

"I love you too." Ray yelled from the back seat.

"You know I love you, baby girl."

****

"Okay, Ms. Henderson, you're all set. We have your tour set up for you, dad, and this little cutie. We can schedule your Lamaze classes the day of the tour. Here, if you have any questions before then, just give us a call." The nurse smiled before she handed Yami a business card.

"Thank you, but I think we're good."

"Do we get to see the babies when we come?" Ray asked.

"Yes, ma'am. You sure do." She smiled at Ray, who was standing next to Yami.

Lena stood in the hall a few feet away listening. Her back was to them while she pretended to look at a flow chart that was on the wall. She was furious about the fact that Yami was here, pregnant, and moving on with her life, like her sister didn't even matter. Miego had killed her sister and was now living his happy new life with his new family, like Kia never existed.

She felt tears forming in her eyes as she looked around, trying to decide what to do. The only thing she could think of forced her to look down at her hands. She was holding a syringe, and instantly knew that she wasn't about to let Yami walk out of there to go on with her happy little life, like her sister's life didn't mean anything.

"Mommy, we get to see the babies," Ray said excitedly, causing both the nurse and Yami to laugh.

"I know, I heard her, Ray." She then focused on the nurse. "Thank you for all your help. I appreciate it."

"No problem, that's what we're here for. Again, feel free to call if you have any questions at all."

"I will."

Yami took her daughter's hand and made her way down the hall with Lena on the move right behind her. She took the stairs because she knew that Yami would recognize her if she got on the elevator with them. Hurrying down, she made it before the elevator arrived and followed Yami and her daughter out the hospital, but not before stealing a scalpel off a tray outside one the rooms she passed, right before they exited the hospital.

As she followed, Lena pulled out her phone and made a quick call, knowing that what she was about to do was going to get her in a lot of trouble.

"Hey, baby, you on break?"

When Jones answered cheerfully, it caused Lena to have second thoughts about attacking Yami. But it only lasted for a second.

"No, but I need your help. I'm about to do something terrible, and I need you to make sure I don't go to jail for it."

"Lena, what are you talking about?" he asked confused.

The two of them were an unlikely pair, but seeing how broken up she was about her sister softened him to her and they formed a connection. That connection continued to grow, and he felt like they were actually getting somewhere. The only problem was her obsession over the death of her sister. Although they were making progress, he knew that she was still struggling with that, and partially blamed him for not being able to make anything stick with Miego.

"That bitch will not just take my sister's place. I'm not gonna let her. You just make sure I don't go to jail for it."

"Lena, wait..."

She hung up and turned her phone off, knowing that he was going to call right back. She couldn't afford any interruptions or for him to try and talk her out of it. She followed Yami and Ray to Yami's car, and just as Yami was reaching into her purse to get her keys out, she yelled at her.

"You stupid bitch. I told you this wasn't over. I guess you though that you could just take my sister's place and nobody would care."

Ray grabbed her mother's leg and moved behind her.

"I'm not even going to waste my time dealing with you. You obviously need help that I can't give you, boo," Yami said once she had her hand on her keys.

She pushed the button to unlock her doors and kept one hand on her daughter.

"Ray, get in."

Ray didn't move though, because of the way Lena was looking at her.

"I don't need you to give me a damn thing, but I have something for you."

Lena pulled the scalpel out of her pocket where she was gripping it with her hand and thrust it into Yami's small protruding belly. Yami immediately doubled over in pain and a rush of panic hit her as her eyes met with her daughter's, who screamed at what she was witnessing.

Lena then took the opportunity to jab the syringe into Yami's neck, which quickly took effect because Yami fell into her car, sliding down it before she hit the ground with Ray yelling and crying by her side.

"Karma is a bitch, ain't it? I hope you bleed to death and I killed that bastard baby," Lena yelled through clenched teeth before she took off running.

Yami was fading, but she managed to keep it together long enough to say one last thing before she lost consciousness. She prayed that her daughter could pull it together enough to follow her instructions.

"Ray, get my phone out my purse. Call Miego and tell him Mommy's hurt."

She was fighting it with everything in her, but her eyes closed and she couldn't seem to stop them, no matter how hard she kept trying. Unfortunately, she was fighting a losing battle and eventually everything went black.

With tears streaming down her face and crying hysterically, Ray cradled against her mother's body and slid her tiny hands into her mother's purse. Once she had her mother's phone, she called Miego but couldn't get the words out.

Hearing her crying had Miego's chest tight, and he was on his feet and moving toward his car. He could hear Train and Memphis yelling behind him, but his focus was on Ray.

"Ray, stop crying, baby girl. What's wrong?"

Through labored breaths and sobs, Ray struggled to speak. Miego felt like time stood still. He was certain that his heart stopped, and the worst feeling in the world followed after he heard Ray's tiny voice.

"Mommy's hurt."

To be continued....
She Fell For A Boss 4: The final Chapter!
Coming Soon!!

Join our mailing list to get a notification when Leo Sullivan Presents has another release!

Text LEOSULLIVAN to 22828 to join!

To submit a manuscript for our review, email us at leosullivanpresents@gmail.com

CPSIA information can be obtained
at www.ICGtesting.com
Printed in the USA
LVOW04s1744021216

515533LV00009B/789/P